C000146016

The Sanctuary Cipher

A dangerous path to ancient treasures,
a cryptic church cipher and priceless
literary works

Jackson Beck

This book was first published in 2020 by KDP

Copyright © Jackson Beck 2020

The right of Jackson Beck to be identified as the Author of this work has been asserted by him in accordance with the Copyright, Designs and Patents Act 1988

ISBN 9798685576613

All rights reserved. No part of this publication may be, reproduced, stored in a retrieval system, or transmitted in any form, or by any means (electronic, mechanical, photocopying, recording or otherwise) without the prior permission of the publisher.

Also, by Jackson Beck

Cabin in the Clouds

Nightfall in Famagusta

Jacksonbeck.com

ST OSWALD'S CHURCH, WINWICK, WARRINGTON

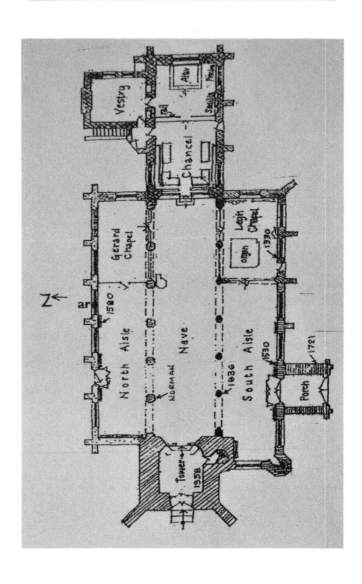

Jacksonbeck.com

Chapter 1

2010 – First Steps

ALEX HELSBY was a run-of-the mill fifty-year-old guy. He stood six feet in height, was of average build and maybe above average intelligence, depending on who you asked. His wife, Karen, was three years younger and eight inches shorter than him. She was known to not suffer fools gladly and worked as a part-time archivist in the Museum of North Cheshire in Warrington. They had two children, Peter who worked for a custodian bank in Manchester, and Louise who was still at high school.

Alex was in business with his brothers, owning a successful locksmith company, Strongarm Devices Limited, just outside Warrington, serving some of the more prosperous areas of the north-west of England. The company had gradually expanded into the installation of some of the latest state-of-the-art access control systems using fingerprint and facial identification. This addition to their portfolio resulted in an increase in their commercial customers and they were now regularly installing systems on some of the industrial estates that surround Manchester Airport and beyond; it was lucrative business.

Alex and his brothers, Derek and Thomas, were equal shareholders in the company, which employed five men on the installation team and two women in the office, who looked after accounts and administration.

Within the company, the brothers had different roles. Derek, the eldest, was a hands-on man who quite often worked on the tools with the installing teams. He was a great problem solver, technically brilliant in his field and never short of new ideas.

Thomas, the middle brother, was the man who carried out quotations, costings and all the on-site surveys. He was the man at the sharp end of all the latest technological requirements of each customer, who needed to keep up to date on current options that were available and, more importantly, he had to be competitive in his proposals.

Alex, the youngest of the three, was more office-inclined so his role oversaw internal procedures, the maintenance of the quality management system, overseeing the accounts, training requirements and anything else that required his attention.

The brothers had worked hard, investing many hours, sometimes at the cost of their comfortable home lives, but it was worth it. They had started the business from their parents' garage thirty-five years ago and hadn't looked back.

Alex was at that age where he was looking for something new in his life – a change, something a bit different. He was still relatively fit for his age and was ready to turn his hand to anything. He had learned how to ski on the snowy slopes of Manchester's indoor venue and had taken up horse riding lessons after watching his daughter learn to ride when she was twelve years old. He had also started jogging and felt much better in himself, even losing a few pounds. As enjoyable as these hobbies were, they didn't really catch his imagination and that was really what he was looking for – something to catch his imagination.

One morning on his way into work, he had heard on Radio Manchester that one of the large universities was starting a community dig, an archaeological dig, which was something he had always fancied. When he got home that evening, he found reference to the community dig on the internet. They were asking for volunteers of any ability or age who were interested in archaeology to apply. All initial training would be given, and on-site tools would be provided. Apparently, the university's Applied Archaeology team had identified six sites throughout Greater Manchester that were worthy of excavation, and money was available to fund the digs for hoardings, materials, toilets etc., and obviously the on-site archaeologists' salaries. Alex spoke briefly to Karen about it; she had no objections and thought it would be a good idea, so he decided to apply. He completed the online application process and emailed it to the relevant department.

Two days later he received a return email thanking him for his application and informing him that he had been successful. The dig was going to be carried out in a public park in Bolton and would include part of the site of the extensive Halliwell Bleach works, which were founded in 1739. He was given a selection of dates. The dig would last for six weeks, and he was being given three days that he could volunteer for, including Saturdays, so he chose the first three Saturdays of the dig duration, completed the form and pressed send.

Within an hour he had a reply informing him that his days had been accepted. He was to report to the dig site at 9.30 a.m. the following Saturday, and should wear stout boots, outdoor clothing, and take along a packed lunch; hot drinks would be provided.

When the first day of his involvement in the dig finally arrived, Alex was feeling a bit anxious about getting to the site on time and having to do something totally new with complete strangers. But he was looking forward to the opportunity and the experience. Unknown to him was that this was to be the first step on a dangerous path, which would eventually lead to his hometown, the finding of ancient treasures, a cryptic church cipher and priceless literary works.

Chapter 2

2018 – Changing Times

TWO YEARS previously the Helsby brothers had decided to sell their family business to a national installer of mechanical and electronic security systems for over £3 million. The brothers had never in their wildest dreams thought that the company could have been worth so much money. It was only after initial interest was shown by a potential purchaser that they consulted their accountant and financial advisors to try to find out what their company was worth.

It came to light that there were several different calculations and formulae to get to the final valuation figure, based on a multiplication of their annual recurring revenue, which in this case was the value of their ongoing maintenance contracts with their clients.

With clients going back over thirty years, most with ongoing contracts, the value of the business was substantial, and the sale of the company, lock, stock and barrel, ensured that the business would continue as a going concern, just under new owners. This was the best solution for the brothers, as it was the most tax efficient way to sell the company, but it also ensured continued employment for their loyal workforce.

Initially the purchaser had suggested that one of the brothers should stay on for a twelve-month handover period, but at the last minute they changed their mind. This meant that the three brothers finished work together at 5 p.m. on a Friday afternoon in June 2016.

Alex was fifty-six years old when he retired, and sometimes he had to pinch himself to make sure that it wasn't a dream and that he was actually financially secure enough to retire at such an early age. He was fortunate and he was thankful.

Although no longer working, the brothers always tried to make a point of getting together every week, which ended up being called the 'Tuesday Club'. It gave them the opportunity to discuss their family issues and interests.

Tuesday Club usually consisted of an activity, such as kayaking or rifle shooting, or quite often a museum or church visit, followed by a pub lunch. The rest of the time the brothers were doing their own thing. Each had a wife, children and their own hobbies and interests.

Ever since Alex's first archaeological dig at Bolton eight years previously he had been totally hooked, and he went on to volunteer for many digs in all areas of the country. He had excavated Roman finds on sites near Hadrian's Wall and in Maryport on the north-west coast of England, and Anglo-Saxon finds on two sites near Oakington in Cambridgeshire. He had joined a local archaeologist and historical group and his interest had been rekindled in his local church of St Oswald's in Winwick.

Winwick is a village on the northern outskirts of Warrington and is separated from the town by the M62 motorway. Not a particularly pretty village, it tends to be driven through rather than stopped at, although it does host a couple of shops, a hairdresser's, a public house and a hotel, which belongs to a national chain – and of course St Oswald's Church.

The village has the M62 on its southern side and the M6 on its eastern flank, while the area to the north of the village is predominantly rural, with arable farming being prominent. To the west and adjacent to the Hollins Park Hospital is quite a large housing estate consisting of everything from apartments to five-bed detached houses.

Although its proximity to the motorway and the general growth of the village is the cause of road congestion at peak times, there are occasions when, in the late evenings and early mornings, it can feel quite rural, especially at certain times of the year when crops are being fertilised or harvested, creating seasonal aromas.

Chapter 3

St Oswald's Church and the Gerard Chapel

ST OSWALD'S Church in Winwick is the centre of the village. It can be seen for miles around like a beacon for Christianity and community life. Directly opposite the church and separated by a narrow driveway known as The Walk, is the church hall and car park.

One Sunday morning in early March 2017 Alex manoeuvred his Toyota Land Cruiser SUV down The Walk and into a parking place directly outside the church hall. He checked the time on the dashboard clock – 9.32 a.m. *Nice and early for the 10 a.m. service. I hope they've fixed the heating*, he thought.

He turned off the engine, applied the handbrake, removed the key and got out of the car. After locking his car, he decided to nip into the hall to see who was in. As he partially opened the door to the hall and stepped in, he was immediately met by a wall of heat. Alex puffed out his cheeks and stepped back to make sure the door stayed open. 'Hello. Anybody in?' he called.

'Just us two again,' came the immediate reply, as Doug and Anne appeared in the doorway from the kitchen.

Doug and Anne were a couple in their eighties who had been involved with the church since their early teens. For the last twenty years or so they had been in charge of the after-service teas, which sometimes included biscuits and cakes. Totally devoted to the church, they thrived on the company of their friends and providing for them in the form of tea.

'Someone has been interfering with the timer, and the heating has been on all night. We've turned it off now, so by the time people come in after the service it won't be too bad,' said Doug.

Alex jokingly mopped his brow. 'I can't take it anymore. I'm going into church. Talk about one extreme to the other.'

Doug and Anne both laughed. 'You may be pleasantly surprised,' Anne said.

Alex walked out of the hall, crossed the car park and went towards the north door of the church. He stopped just for a second and looked up in amazement at the church bell tower and spire in all its sandstone glory, circa 1350. *It still amazes me every time I see it. I must check the church clock weights to see if it needs winding.*

The lantern above the heavy outer door was illuminated, indicating that the church was open. The north door would originally have been the rear entrance but was now favoured because the pathways were better, and it was simpler to get to the church hall and car park.

Alex walked through the open heavy outer door and pushed the inner door, which complained with a low creaking noise. He was met by Janice Wainwright, the churchwarden, a lovely woman who had been warden for twenty years. She was always smart in appearance and although sixty years old, had the appearance of a woman ten years younger.

'Good morning Alex,' Janice said.

'Morning,' he replied.

'Everything okay?' she asked.

'All good thanks. The back's a bit stiff but ...'

'You've been digging again.'

'Of course. What else is a retired man supposed to do?'

'Where this time?'

'With my digging partner Dave in a farmer's field near Leyland.'

'Any luck?'

'Oh just a few bits and pieces ... you know.'

'That's what you always say.'

'Well I don't want the wrong type to know that my house is bulging with jewels and precious metals,' Alex said, giving her a wink. Janice turned up her nose and pretended to walk away.

'If you're really interested,' Alex added, 'I'll tell you all about it over coffee in the church hall afterwards.'

Janice did two small excited claps. 'I'd like that.'

'I'm just going to check the clock weights, to see if it needs winding up.'

'Okay,' Janice replied.

Alex walked towards the rear of the church and the tower, thinking to himself. *Thank goodness the heating is on. I was half expecting it to be like a fridge in here. I could do with putting my back against one of the radiators to loosen it up a little. I do hope this clock doesn't need winding up again, as I don't fancy staying after church, especially now I've promised Janice.*

He walked past the stone font and peered into the area that was the domain of the bell ringers, who

22

were due any minute. Alex could see that the steel counterweights were still very high. He reckoned on at least another four days before they hit the floor. The clock winder Mark would be back from holiday before then, so he wouldn't need to fill in for him.

The inside of the tower was an impressive space. One of the two original parts of the church, dating back to 1350, its solid sandstone walls of approximately one metre in thickness created an internal area of seven and a half square metres, and it was fifteen metres in height to the clock room timber floor.

Through this timber floor hung six heavy ropes, each one attached to the clapper of its own eighteenth century cast bell, which were fixed to a pivoted beam, called the headstock, enabling them to swing. The bell ropes connected to the clappers via a wheel attached to the headstock. The ropes travelled down the clock tower, originating in the belfry, through the clock room and down into the bell ringers' domain.

There were two other smaller ropes, one for disengaging the clappers, on very rare occasions, and the other one for ringing a smaller bell known as the chantry bell. In 1600 this bell was dedicated to the memory of some of the church's wealthier patrons, such as Peter Legh, Thomas Gerard, Edward Eccleston, Edward Stanley, Thomas Stanley and John Rider.

The clock was installed in 1876, being hand wound using a large handle twice a week. The two winding mechanisms on the clock raised the counterweights, then gravity did the rest.

Alex walked back into the nave, the main area of the church, as more people entered for the 10 a.m. Holy Communion. He walked to the table near the entrance and picked up his hymn book, pew news and service sheet for the day. After greeting a few of the other parishioners, he sat in a pew near the rear of the church and closed his eyes to say to himself his morning prayer:

Almighty and everlasting God, I thank you that you have brought me safely to the beginning of this day. Keep me from falling into sin or running into danger. Order me in all my doings and guide me to do always what is righteous in your sight. Through Jesus Christ our Lord. Amen.

The service was seamless, without interruption, concluding at 11 a.m. The Reverend Jill Chaplow reached the north door in the closing procession, preceded by the crucifer, who happened to be Doug. The crucifer's role was to carry the church processional cross, and Alex was one of a team of four on a rota who performed this task. The vicar waited by the open door as people filed past, shaking her hand and thanking her for a lovely service and sermon. Doug made his way back to the vestry, crucifer duties complete.

Alex was exchanging pleasantries with a couple of ladies when he noticed that the plates with the collection money were still on the altar. He decided that he would take the money into the vestry to count it before he went over to the church hall. As a member of the church council he was permitted to do this as part of his responsibility within the church.

He was part of another rota, which included being a sidesperson, which involved giving hymn books out and the taking around of the collection plate during the service. This was his day off from the rota, but he just couldn't help getting involved. He walked through the nave, took the collection plates, then walked through the chancel and into the vestry. Doug was already there, having placed the cross in its holding bracket, and he was removing his alb, a white cassock-type garment with a cincture rope-type belt.

'That went well,' said Alex.

'Yes, it certainly did. I reckon the children lift the atmosphere, even if some elders shake their heads at the slightest noise from them,' Doug replied, feeding a clothes hanger through his alb before hanging it in the wardrobe.

'I agree,' replied Alex, as he placed the plates of money and cash on to the vestry table.

'Do you need a hand with the counting?' asked Doug.

'No, I'll be fine. You get over to the hall before the catering corps send out a search party. I'll follow you over in about ten minutes.'

'Okay,' Doug said, as he left the vestry in a hurry.

Alex started to count the money, firstly by separating the offertory envelopes on to one plate, and all the cash on to the other. *I think I'll wait a few minutes for someone else to come in and corroborate these cash amounts.* So, Alex sat back in the chair and looked around the vestry, shaking his head. *It's getting untidy again, boxes everywhere.*

Later, having finished with the money, Alex was enjoying a coffee and a chocolate biscuit in the church hall with Janice. 'Come on then, tell me what you've been up to,' she said.

'Well, my friend Dave, who I don't think you've met, although I've shown him around the church, is in an archaeological group in his home town of Chorley. They asked whether I could give them a hand on the dig that has just revealed artefacts from under that proposed new shopping centre. The development has been put on hold for another week, until they get satisfactory answers to explain the number of skeletons they've found on a greenfield site.'

'That's amazing. And how old do they think the skeletons are?'

'Potentially seventeenth century,' said Alex, 'and that's based upon other items they've excavated and the site's location, which is believed to be an English Civil War site.'

'That's really fascinating. So, are you back there again tomorrow?' Janice asked.

'No, I really need to rest my back, it's getting worse. I was thinking of having a couple of months off and away from digging. Dave will keep me informed about how the dig is going and what's being found.'

The couple were then interrupted by another member of the congregation, Les Pritchard, a local landowner and farmer. In his mid-sixties, he was still a very fit man, with salt and pepper, thin hair, but standing at least six feet three inches tall. He was still very physically active, and his huge hands, although generally clean, were engrained with dirt and oil, and a couple of the ends of his fingers looked badly cracked, probably due to working outside and in the elements.

'Excuse me,' Les interjected, 'I couldn't help overhearing, and it caught my attention when you mentioned the Civil War.'

'Why's that then?' asked Alex.

'Well, we've just been notified that a lot of our farmland is being listed as a battlefield site from the English Civil War.'

'Listed by who?' enquired Alex.

'The English Civil War Society apparently. Well that's the name all over the documents I've just received.'

'What does that mean for you Les? Are there any restrictions as to what you can do with your land?' Alex asked him.

'There doesn't seem to be. Unless I'm building an estate of houses, which I'm not. But to be quite honest I haven't really read all the information; I've just briefly glanced through it and looked at the plans.'

'Plans?' enquired Alex. 'Plans for what?'

'Well, I say plans ... it's like a map of the area that they've produced and then shaded in the areas that are included in the listing.'

'Is the church and hall included on the listing?' asked Alex.

'Yes, I think it is. If you're that interested give me a call in the morning and come around to my farm. You can gladly have a look at the paperwork.'

'I'll do that, and thanks Les. I'll see you tomorrow.'

'Okay,' Les replied, making towards the exit.

Alex turned to Janice, who had been listening to the conversation. 'That was interesting,' she said, 'but I hope you're not thinking about starting your own archaeological dig, particularly after what you said about having a few months away from digging.'

Alex smiled. 'I know, but I'd like to see the information on the battlefield site and then I'll ask my back how it's feeling.'

The hall door opened, and Reverend Jill walked in, approaching Alex and Janice with a meaningful step. 'I'm so sorry, but could one of you, or both of you preferably, deal with a small group of American tourists. I think they're looking for a guided tour, but unfortunately I have to leave now to make some home visits and to give communion in the nursing home.'

Alex and Janice stood up simultaneously. 'Yes, no problem,' said Alex. 'I'll just have to let Karen know I'm running late.'

Janice echoed his sentiments, then they were both texting their spouses. 'I'm so grateful,' said Jill.

As Alex and Janice walked up the path towards the north door of the church there was a small group of people in a cluster by the door. They looked like tourists. One or two were carrying small backpacks, and six of the eight were carrying quite substantial and expensive-looking SLR cameras.

Janice approached the door. 'Good morning everyone.'

'Good morning,' came the combined reply with the distinctive American accent. As soon as Janice took the key from her handbag there was an audible 'wow' from some of the visitors. She held up the key, which was a good eight inches in length and was a traditional key shape of solid steel construction.

'I know, it's pretty impressive isn't it. The last time we had a new key made it cost £100, which was a bit of a shock, so I guard it with my life.' The visitors smiled then filed through the door, with Alex taking up the rear.

Janice made her way to the vestry to collect their guided tour notes while Alex sat the visitors down in the central front pews and issued a welcome booklet to each person. He then put two stand-alone chairs together on the slightly raised platform area, as Janice joined him with the guide notes, and they faced the visitors.

'Good morning everyone and welcome to St Oswald's. My name is Alex and my colleague is Janice. Now Janice is a very important member of our church. Not only is she a keyholder for the main north door but she's also our churchwarden, so when Reverend Jill is away, Janice is the boss. Now, as you can see, Janice is quite a fearsome character so we must do what she says.' Janice blushed and some of the visitors laughed as Alex put his arm around her tiny frame.

Janice gathered her composure with a smile, pointing at the entrance door. 'If we need to leave the church in an emergency, please use the north door, which is the one that we've just entered through. If anyone needs the toilets, go through the same door and they're situated in the church hall opposite, which is the white building. I'll just hand you back to Alex.'

Alex continued the instructions. 'What we intend is to walk around the church as a group and you just ask questions as we go, but please bear in mind we're not historians, we're history enthusiasts, so we may not have the answers to all of your questions.

'Now you probably noticed on your approach that the church is built on quite a prominent piece of walled land. This has led historians to believe that there may have been numerous religious buildings on this site prior to the commencement of this current church in 1358, and as you'll see shortly, we retain part of a tenth century Anglo-Saxon cross that was recovered from the churchyard.

'In the Domesday book of 1086 there's reference to St Oswald's Church on this site, and a couple of other facts for you: this is a Grade 1 Listed building, which means it's highly regarded as a building of high historical value. This church also sits within the boundaries of the English Civil War battlefield of 1648 and as such is listed as a battlefield site.' At this point one of the visitors raised his hand. 'Yes?' said Alex.

An elderly man with a grey beard and what looked like a small stud in one of his ears stood up. 'I was wondering where the name St Oswald came from.'

'Okay,' said Janice, 'there's an explanation on the back page of your welcome booklet, but briefly, Oswald was born in the year 604 and his father was the King of Northumbria. When his father was killed in battle, Oswald and his brothers fled to Scotland and, at some point, Oswald spent some time at the monastery on the island of Iona and became a Christian.

'In 633 Oswald returned to Northumbria to claim his crown upon the death of the king. To cut a long story short, Oswald eventually secured his kingdom and began to spread the word of Christianity across the region along with his trusted missionary Aidan and began to establish churches. As a result, Oswald granted Aidan and his followers the island of Lindisfarne.'

A couple in the group were now nodding in recognition of the island, also known as Holy Island, as Janice continued. 'They founded a monastery on Lindisfarne, which I suspect you've all heard of.' Cue more nods and a communal 'yes' from the visitors.

Janice had captivated her audience; this was, after all, her specialist subject and she had been to Lindisfarne on many occasions. 'Unfortunately, after eight years as King of Northumbria, Oswald was killed in battle and it's said that various parts of his body were dispatched to locations within his kingdom; however, his head is now buried with St Cuthbert in Durham Cathedral.

'Oswald is recognised as one of England's foremost Anglo-Saxon Christian kings, and legend has it that he had a palace at Woodhead in Winwick and that he died nearby at the village of Hermitage Green, where a well, now known as St Oswald's Well, sprung up after his death. The well is situated at Woodhead Farm, which is also infamous for a more modern piece of English history. Are there any questions?'

Janice's words were drowned out by a few seconds of spontaneous applause and she blushed again. Alex thought to himself: S*he deserves that, she loves the topic, but I bet some of these visitors know more than us.*

One of the female visitors was holding up her hand. 'Excuse me, you mentioned that Oswald is believed to have been killed nearby. If his base is in Northumbria am I not right in thinking that's a fair distance from here? I believe further to the north?'

'Yes, you're correct but this area was also part of his kingdom and it's said that he fell in the battle of Masefield. We have a town only a few miles away called Ashton-in-Makerfield and it's believed to be the same location … by some but not all,' Janice explained.

The woman appeared to be happy with the explanation, then held up her hand again. 'Excuse me again. I'm sorry.'

'No, its fine,' assured Janice.

'You mentioned … Woodhead Farm was it?'

'Yes.'

'And that it's connected to a piece of more modern English history. Can you tell us about that?'

Janice looked at Alex. 'Would you like to take it from here?'

'Certainly,' said Alex. 'If you can please follow me to the Gerard Chapel.' Alex gesticulated towards the area to his right.

Situated in the north-east corner of the north aisle, the Gerard Chapel is now used as an historical area within the church. In the east wall is a beautiful stained-glass window dedicated to the Stone family. The window depicts King Oswald in full armour erecting a Christian cross on the ancient battlefield of Havenfield in Northumbria. The other images show the king experiencing a Christian vision and distributing food and valuables to the poor. Either side of this window there are two exquisite oil paintings of former rectors. To the left is Reverend

Charles Herle, who was the incumbent in 1626, and to the right is Reverend Richard Sherlock, who was the incumbent in 1660 and can be seen with a copy of his book *Practical Christian*. Both men are shown in their respective religious dress of the day complete with their Canterbury black caps.

The visitors followed Alex and Janice into the Gerard Chapel and Alex now ventured into his specialist subject, pointing out a small standing sign that asked people not to stand on the brass.

'The sign refers to the large brass flat monument representing Sir Piers Gerard of Bryn, a noted Roman Catholic family man who died in 1495. The figure of the brass knight is engraved in a tabard bearing a crowned rampant lion. The local seat of the Gerards was a moated hall at Bryn, a village not too far away from Winwick. It was at various times a refuge for hunted priests in the days of persecution and religious intolerance.

'One of Sir Piers's descendants, Father John Gerard, is famous for managing to escape from the

Tower of London on 5 October 1597 and went on to be implicated in the Gunpowder Plot of 1605. Fortunately, Father Gerard recorded his memoirs and went on to write *The Autobiography of a Hunted Priest*, which is still read by scholars and enthusiasts today.

'Other notable members of the Gerard dynasty, such as Richard born in 1613, and in particular his older brother Thomas, went on to be early settlers in Maryland in the US.

'If you gather around, you'll see here a piece of the modern history mentioned earlier.' Alex was pointing at a framed document that hung on the north wall. 'This is a copy of a marriage certificate from 1887 when Edward John Smith, the captain of the Titanic, married Sarah Eleanor Pennington from Woodhead Farm in Winwick in this very church.'

The visitors looked shocked. They never expected this. 'Can we take photographs?' someone asked.

'Of course,' replied Alex.

'So, his wife was from the Woodhead Farm, where St Oswald's Well is situated?' asked one of the visitors.

'Yes,' confirmed Janice. 'It's an amazing coincidence.'

'We had no idea of the Titanic connection to this church,' stated one of the visitors, 'and the history of the Gerards and the Tower of London. Not to mention the Gunpowder Plot.'

'We're not the best at publicising our assets,' said Alex, 'and we've only just started. We'll leave you at this point to have a look around and take photographs. Please refer to your welcome booklet, or if you have any questions please don't hesitate to ask.'

There were many questions, and many photographs were taken. The cross head of a tenth century Anglo-Saxon cross, the fourteenth century sandstone font and, of course, the brass memorial to Sir Piers Gerard were all big hits with the visitors, and these were just some of the items in the Gerard Chapel.

Suddenly the visitors seemed to form into their familiar huddle, then one of the group, a stout woman in her fifties, approached Alex and Janice. 'I'm very sorry but we're going to have to leave shortly, as we're cruising from Liverpool early evening back to the States. It's the last leg of our holiday.'

'Oh, that sounds fantastic,' said Janice. 'I've never been on a cruise.'

'I can recommend it,' said the woman. 'Just like I'll be recommending a visit to this church when I get back. I work in the tourism industry and this is a place our country folk should be visiting. We'd like to donate £50 to the church.' She handed over the money to Janice.

'Oh, that's so kind. Thank you,' replied Janice.

'Yes, thank you so much,' added Alex. 'And if we could exchange contact details, I can keep you in touch with any developments here in the church.'

'Yes, I'd like that,' the woman replied.

After the visitors from the US had left, Janice and Alex felt a sense of achievement about their visit. 'What lovely people,' said Alex.

'Yes, they were, and so enthusiastic. I wish we'd had time to talk to them about the Legh Chapel, the Norman stone heads, the Pugin Chancel and all the other things,' said Janice.

'Well, hopefully we've created a good enough impression that maybe one or two of them will revisit us in the future.' Alex looked at the business card the visitor had given to him. 'Or that maybe Erin White, who just so happens to be Overseas Sales Director, will maybe make us big news in the States.' Alex and Janice did a high-five. It was so unlike them, but they did it anyway.

That evening after dinner Alex retired to his study. The events from earlier in the day had prompted him to open his box files on the Gerards. His fascination with this aristocratic family was considerable. He had ploughed through hours and hours of their family tree on different genealogy websites and had made good contacts in the US following one particular line of the family.

They were one of the many prominent Catholic families from the locality and the sixteenth and seventeenth centuries were an era of particular interest. The slightest hint of an association with the Gunpowder Plot was the initial trigger. Alex was reading an extraction from one of the genealogy websites.

Father John Gerard SJ (Society of Jesus) was born in 1564. He was the second son of Sir Thomas Gerard of Bryn, who was imprisoned in the Tower of London in 1569 for plotting the rescue of Mary Queen of Scots. John and his brother, Thomas, were located in a friend's household until their father was released three years later.

John and his brother were sent to Exeter College in Oxford but stayed barely a year due to pressures applied to force the students to attend church and receive the Protestant sacrament. Their tutor at Oxford accompanied the Gerard boys home with the intention of becoming a Catholic and to continue tutoring them.

In 1577 John attended the Douai seminary in Rheims, France, where he stayed for three years and decided to enter the Society of Jesus.

After a year at the Jesuit school at Clermont in Paris he decided to return to England after a serious illness in 1583. When his ship landed at Dover, John was arrested by the customs officials and imprisoned at Marshalsea Prison in south London. John is said to have described the prison as having so many Catholics that it was like a school of Christ.

A year later John was released after a bond payment by Anthony Babington, who was subsequently executed for his own attempt to release Mary Queen of Scots.

John found safety in Rome, where he entered the English College and eventually received a papal dispensation to complete his noviceship in England.

John left for England with Fathers Oldcorne, Bales and Beesley, all three of whom were later executed for their faith. The situation for Catholics in England was diabolical as their persecution continued. However, John quickly created the right impression and developed a strong following amongst the Catholic gentry. He was, though, a wanted man, and as such was moved regularly from location to location, sometimes evading capture by minutes with the use of priest holes and secret hideaways.

John's luck ran out on 23 April 1594 when he was finally captured. A short while later he was imprisoned in the Tower of London, where he was tortured to reveal the names and locations of some of his fellow Catholics.

'They took me to a big upright pillar, one of the posts which held the roof of this huge underground chamber. Driven into the top of it were iron staples for supporting heavy weights. Then they put my wrists into iron gauntlets and ordered me to climb two or three wicker steps. My arms were then lifted up and an iron bar passed through the rings of one gauntlet, then through the staple and rings of the second gauntlet. This done, they fastened the bar with a pin to prevent it slipping, and then removing the wicker steps one by one from under my feet, they left me hanging by my hands and arms fastened above my head.'

When asked if he would like to confess, he did of course refuse.

'Such a gripping pain came over me. It was worst in my chest, belly, hands and arms. All the blood in my body seemed to rush up into my arms and hands and I thought that blood was oozing out from

the ends of my fingers and the pores of my skin.'

He was hung like this for several hours, only relieving the pressure on his arms when he fainted. He was tortured on three separate occasions without revealing anything.

Pending his trial John had contrived his escape from the Tower with a system of secret letters and signals. On 4 October 1597, they fastened a rope from a tower across the moat, the rope being almost horizontal, so they had to inch their way along the rope to safety. John, still being weak from torture, barely made it across but was soon safe in the hands of his friends and fled the vicinity by boat. Taking a horse provided for him he fled to the home of Robert Catesby.

John went on to convert many to the Catholic cause, including Sir Everard Digby. Catesby and Digby were two of many who conspired against Parliament to form the Gunpowder Plot. Once the plot was discovered a proclamation was issued against Gerard and others, forcing him into even deeper hiding. With the aid of his friends and a suitable disguise he was able to leave the country. He lived the rest of his life quietly under the wing of the Jesuits. In 1637 at the age of 73 he died in Rome.

John's father Sir Thomas Gerard had died in 1601 and was buried at St Oswald's Church, Winwick on 28 October of that year.

John's nephews, Richard and Dr Thomas Gerard, went on to be early adventurers in the New World at Maryland. Richard sailed on The Ark and The Dove with the Calverts in 1634 and Thomas followed him to settle in Virginia in 1638. The following year Thomas was commissioned the Lord of the Manor at St Clement's in Maryland. His family joined him in 1650. He died in Virginia in 1673. Richard only lasted a year before returning home to England to become a distinguished soldier. He died in 1686.

By this time, Alex's eyes were tired of reading. It was late and time for bed. Another busy day was planned for tomorrow. He slept well that night.

Chapter 4

Alex's First Find

THE FOLLOWING day Alex called Les Pritchard and arrived at his farm in his beloved SUV just before noon. Alex approached the large imposing seventeenth century L-shaped house from the front driveway, which, in fashion with most farmhouses, was quite muddy and rutted in places.

As he pulled to a stop a quantity of mud and water was forced out from beneath the front nearside tyre, hitting the front porch window with considerable force. Alex got out of the car and approached the side door of the porch just as Les opened the door.

'I heard you coming,' Les said.

Alex blushed. 'Oh, I'm sorry about the mess on your window.'

'No, not that,' Les said. 'I could hear your car a mile off. Is your exhaust blowing or something?'

'Erm, I don't think so. It's always been very throaty.' *Probably due to the 4.4 litre turbo diesel engine and sports exhaust system, which is how it came; but not worth going into that now*, thought Alex.

Les invited Alex in. 'Come through to the kitchen and leave your boots on the mat in front of you. I don't mind mud on the drive as long as that's where it stays.'

'No problem,' said Alex, removing his all-weather-style walking boots.

They sat down at a large pine traditional-looking farmhouse table; the heavy chairs scraped along the tiled kitchen floor as they were moved into position. Les pulled some documents out of a large white envelope and fanned them out on the table in front of him.

'These are the documents I was telling you about Alex. You can have a look through them. Do you want a tea or coffee?'

'Er, coffee please … white no sugar.'

'Okay,' said Les as he got up from the table.

Alex looked at the documents in front of him, all headed 'ENGLISH CIVIL WAR SOCIETY'. There was a formal covering letter, which basically explained the contents of the envelope. Amongst other official-looking documents Alex noticed a grid reference map with areas that had been highlighted. Then another map, this one of the ordnance survey type covering the whole of the north Warrington area, which clearly showed the extent of the battlefield site in a different shade and explaining that the battle was known as the battle of Red Bank or Winwick Pass, taking place on 19 August 1648. It culminated in the end of the Second Civil War and the defeat of the Royalists.

The area shown on the ordnance survey map was in the form of a triangle positioned upside down with

St Oswald's right at the bottom point. The area then projected north, roughly following Moorsdale Lane and Winwick Lane, including the land between these roads and on either side; they finished approximately one mile away near the area called Red Bank. Red Bank was shown on the map with the crossed swords symbol of a battlefield site.

Alex then took a closer look at the grid reference map, which appeared to show field boundaries, woods, streams and trackways. He held up the map and showed it to Les. 'Is the area that's highlighted your land Les?'

Les walked over and positioned his spectacles from the loop around his neck. 'Yes, that's right, the other fields around it used to be ours but I've sold them over the years.'

Alex looked at the map until he had worked out which fields he was looking at and roughly where they were. One of the fields was positioned roughly in the middle of the battlefield and to the West of Moorsdale Lane; the smaller field was positioned further south and nearer to the church. Alex thought that both were prime sites where you would expect some remains from any fighting, particularly metallic, to still be in situ.

Les returned to the table with two mugs of coffee and placed them on the table between the gaps in the documents.

'Thanks, Les,' said Alex. 'Just going back to these two fields of yours. The larger field to the north … what would you call it?'

'It's known as Moors Field, always has been, and the field nearer to the church is Claybarn Field.'

'And what do you use them for Les?'

'Barley, both fields.'

'What condition are they in now?'

'Well they were harvested last September, and they've been ploughed and planted for this year's growth.'

Alex looked at the map and then turned to Les. 'Would you give me access to these fields?'

'I knew you would be interested, but it depends what you're going to do. If you want to dig thirty-metre trenches, one metre deep like that crowd of archaeologists on the TV, forget it.'

'No,' said Alex, smiling, 'definitely not. In the first instance I'd like to do a bit of field walking, to see what's on the surface.'

'Be my guest. As long as we agree on any finds.'

'What would you like to agree?'

Les shuffled uncomfortably in his seat, then said, 'A fifty-fifty split.'

'That sounds fair enough, but I'd like to display some finds in the church, especially anything Civil War-related,' suggested Alex.

'That's a great idea. How long have you been interested in history and archaeology and all that stuff?'

'Well, a number of years really. I've travelled to different parts of the country following digs or research, but never really looked at my hometown. I knew the area had some Roman history and that the

English Civil war had played a part, but until I looked at these documents, I didn't realise how big and what an impact the war in particular had on this area. I certainly never realised its potential from an archaeological point of view.'

'I think it's the same for a lot of folk,' said Les. 'It's only, say, the last five years or so that certain people have been pushing hard to have the area listed as a battlefield site. You'll notice that it says on the covering letter that there are no additional lawful controls on the land, but any planning applications would be scrutinised because of the listing, so it won't make any difference to us. I'll be quite honest with you though Alex, I've had people on those fields before … you know … metal detectorists, and they haven't found much. Not that they would tell me if they had anyway.'

'I would,' replied Alex.

'I know,' said Les knowingly as they shook hands, smiling and firmly looking each other in the eye.'

Alex continued, 'If I do find anything considered old or of value, I'd also like to inform the local finds liaison officer at the portable antiquities scheme. They're the authority on archaeological finds and usually want to know about anything found that's considered older than AD 1700, or contains precious metals or gemstones. It's just the right thing to do Les, battlefield site or not.'

'No one has ever mentioned this organisation to me before, but I presumed there would be some kind of system in place. I haven't got a problem with that Alex. You go ahead and do what you're going to do, but no trenches.'

'I get the message. I'll have to get the cobwebs off my metal detector.'

Alex arrived home with the copies of the documents that Les had provided. He took his boots off and placed them on a mat in the hall cupboard and closed the door. He went upstairs to his study, lifted his laptop lid and pressed the on button. He went straight to Google Earth to take a good view of the fields and the area between Winwick's church and Red Bank.

As he looked at the overhead view of Moors Field, he focused in. He could see a dark patch of woods in the middle of the field; the rest of it was straw-coloured, looking as if the photograph had been taken before the harvest. It looked like any other field in the summer, warm and welcoming, and you could almost smell the crops and imagine the skylark's melody in the air. You would never have known that many people were slaughtered in battle in these fields over three hundred and fifty years ago.

Alex withdrew the focus slightly to take in the overall view again, before concentrating on Claybarn Field. This was a smaller square field, similar in colour to Moors Field, and surrounded on three sides by trees or hedgerows. It was about a quarter of a mile further south towards the church. *I wonder what these fields look like now in early March. I think I'll drive down there this afternoon and take a look.*

Alex picked up the document envelope that Les had given him and began to read the page entitled 'DESCRIPTION OF MILITARY ACTION'.

On 18 August 1648, the day after the battle of Preston, it is believed that 7,000 infantry and 4,000 mounted troops of Royalists and Scots were pursued by Oliver Cromwell's New Model Army of Parliamentarians. Cromwell's army numbered about 6,000 infantry and 2,500 mounted troops. Just north of Wigan the Royalists made as if to stand and fight, before retiring to the town where they spent the night plundering, despite the town's Royalist sympathies. The following day the battle comprised of an initial stand by several regiments of Royalists followed by their fighting retreat. The Royalists decided to make a stand at Red Bank just outside Winwick but ended up retreating up the hill to Winwick's church; their cries for mercy were heard for many a mile.

After a bloody battle, killing in excess of 1,000, it is claimed that anything between 1,000 and 2,000 Royalist prisoners were placed under guard at St Oswald's Church, before being stripped of their weapons and valuables and force-marched into Warrington. This was to signal the beginning of the end of the Second English Civil War.

Alex hadn't realised that it had occurred on this scale and the report went on to say that the area is the only Civil War battlefield to survive in a good state of preservation. Alex just knew he had to have a closer look, so he picked up the maps and went downstairs. With his boots and coat on he was back in the SUV and on his way to Winwick.

As Alex drove past the church, he was aware of the location of Claybarn Field, which he was just about to pass, but his attention had been drawn to Moors Field and that was where he was heading. A minute later he was taking a sharp left turn off Moorsdale Lane into Moors Field.

This was an open entrance to the field through a gap in the hedgerow, which all the tractors and other farm vehicles would use. It was in a very poor state, just a sea of mud and water, but Alex could see that the field changed for the better just a few metres in. With wheels spinning and mud flying he was through the entrance and on the trackway at the foot of the field. He slid to a halt and got out. *What an amazingly beautiful view that you just can't see from the road*, he thought.

The whole of the field was dark soil in furrow formation sloping up the hill towards a small copse of trees, which looked as if they had fallen from the sky and had been ploughed and worked around for ever. The view was spectacular and stretched across more fields and nearby towns and villages.

Alex started to walk along the perimeter of the field near the hedgerow, heading north. This hedgerow was so thick that he couldn't see through it, but he could vaguely see images of cars flashing by. It felt so private yet so open.

Alex put his head down and started his field walk. Field walking can be a good indication of what lies beneath; quite often pieces from historical sites are revealed by ploughing equipment turning over the earth. Consequently, this year's reveal could be ploughed back into the deep earth the following year, like a continuous cycle.

As Alex walked along the perimeter adjacent to the road, he came across the usual items tossed out of or falling from passing vehicles – empty cans, bottles, bolts, exhaust pipes, hub caps and general rubbish. When he reached a large tree, which appeared to be approximately halfway up the field, he decided to turn west towards the centre of the field. The mud stuck to his boots, and instead of walking up the hill in the furrows, he was now walking across at ninety degrees.

It was noticeable that there were wet areas of soil, and even wetter areas that were holding water in the furrows. There was less evidence of litter and rubbish here at least. In fact, the quality of the soil was very good, it just happened to be the type of stuff that stuck to your boots and bottoms of your trousers. Consequently, his boots got bigger and bigger and heavier and heavier.

He stopped in the centre of the field and realised he was starting to ache. He rubbed the base of his back. *I wouldn't be able to dig in this, it's too heavy and wet. I'd do myself more harm than good.*

He turned another ninety degrees and headed back in the general direction of his SUV. Eyes glued to the floor he came across a couple of recently spent modern shotgun cartridges, with a red sheath and a brass-coloured end cap. *There's probably a rabbit problem here; I noticed quite a few burrows near the hedgerow.*

Alex continued at a slow walk, wondering what it was like out here in the middle of this field in 1648, running for your life, with the fear of being shot in the back by a musket ball or being caught by your enemy. Something caught his eye a couple of paces ahead, lying on the surface, nearly white in colour. *Looks like a clay pipe stem*.

He bent down and picked it up, moving it around his hand and fingers. He looked for the telltale black spot at each end of the stem, and sure enough there they were; that was the hole which ran the length of the stem in which the smoke was drawn through. *Nice little piece of clay pipe but without a bowl; almost impossible to date. My first find though.*

Pipes made of clay had been introduced to the UK in the late sixteenth century, compliments of Virginia Tobacco from the New World and Sir Walter Raleigh. Although worthless, Alex dropped the piece of clay pipe into his jacket pocket. It meant something to him. He carried on his field walk and within a couple of metres he had found another small piece of pipe, then another and another. He had recovered four pieces of pipe in a very small area and as his eyes scanned the ground around him, he could see more. He collected them and they all went into his jacket pocket.

From that area of about four-square metres he eventually found seventeen small pieces of clay pipe, all similar in size and colour. He gathered some of the small rocks and stones that were lying about and made a mound about twelve inches high as his marker. He continued his walk back to the vehicle, still scanning the soil; he found no further pieces of clay pipe.

On his way home he decided to call in at the rectory. Reverend Jill answered the door in her black trousers, long-sleeved clergy shirt and clerical collar.

'Sorry, are you just on your way out?' Alex asked.

'No, I've just come in. Today is an afternoon of administration, but please come in. You're always welcome.'

Alex slipped off his boots and left them on the mat outside before stepping in. 'Thanks Jill. I know you're very busy.'

'Don't be silly; come into the study.' Alex walked through to the study, which was at the rear of the rectory.

The house was quite large and stood in extensive gardens. There were no borders full of plants and rockeries, it was mainly laid to lawn, with an occasional shrub hedge and a couple of large attractive sycamore trees, which produced thousands of seeds, the type which you throw into the air and they rotate to the ground like a helicopter blade. Positioned pretty centrally in the village, it was a five-minute walk to church. Owned by the Diocese of the Church of England, the house was maintained to a good standard by certain members of the congregation who were skilled in the relevant trades.

The walls in the study were covered in shelves, a number of which held box files with descriptions of their contents written on the outer edge in dark, heavy lettering. There were also books, lots of books, based on religion, a collection of bibles, old and new, novels, biographies, and a collection of historical books that the local mobile library couldn't surpass.

The study window gave a framed view of a manicured lawn as the spring sunshine shone through tree branches, projecting a dappled reflection on to the opposite wall. It gave the room a warm feeling. There were two high-back office swivel chairs on casters and Jill pulled one over for Alex.

'Would you like a drink?' she asked.

'I'll have a glass of your famous flavoured water if you have any.'

'As it happens, I have.' She left the room and went to the kitchen. *If it's as nice as last time I must ask her where she gets it from*, Alex thought to himself.

Jill returned and presented Alex with a tumbler full of cloudy water. He took a taste and thought it tasted even better this time. 'Jill, where do you get this water from?'

'Oh, it's just tap water that I flavour with lemon and lime, put it through a strainer and leave to cool in the fridge.'

'Well I have an idea. You should go into business selling St Oswald's finest spring water; it would be good for the church.'

'But not good for me, unless I'm given a curate solely for that purpose.' They both laughed.

'So how is Karen doing?' Jill asked.

'Very well thanks; still working at the museum and still loving it.'

'So, what are your plans for today?'

'Well, I called in at the Pritchard's this morning, then I went to Moors Field.'

'Oh, how are the Pritchards? I didn't really get chance to speak to them after the service.'

'Les is fine. I didn't see Annie, but I just had an interesting meeting with him about the English Civil War battlefield and his land,' Alex said excitedly.

'Of course, he owns most of the battlefield,' said Jill. 'In fact, we're sitting in the middle of the battlefield now, just like the church and both churchyards.'

'I only realised yesterday and have seen it on a map today. I take it that you've had a similar notification to Les?' Alex asked.

'I've received several documents from the English Civil War Society that give information, and an ordnance survey map of the battlefield.'

'Yes, that sounds the same.'

'I know you have an interest in archaeology. Is it your plan to do some excavation work Alex?'

'Well not exactly. I'm planning to do some metal detecting and as little digging as possible.'

'Is that because of your back?'

'I'm afraid so. I was wondering whether you had any papers or books on the battle of Red Bank so that I can familiarise myself with what actually occurred.'

'Yes, I have some books here that you can take away with you and I'll email you some links to websites that I believe the English Civil War Society used in the production of their report.'

'That would be fantastic Jill, thank you so much.'

'I should imagine Moors Field would be a great place for you to start and I presume that there have never been any buildings on it. From what I've read, after the battle at Red Bank there were further running battles in the surrounding fields.'

'I feel very hopeful about it, although Les informed me that there have been people metal detecting in his fields in the past.'

'Still worth a go though,' Jill replied.

'Oh yes, and if I find anything of interest, I'd like to display it in the Gerard Chapel, if that's okay with you.'

'Yes, that would be fine. It could only enhance the historical aspect of the church, as long as there are no bones.'

'I promise not to retrieve any bones.' Alex smiled, wondering why he had just thought about Scooby Doo.

Jill retrieved two books from the shelf behind her. 'These are very good reference books if you're interested in the whole of the Civil War and the different battles that occurred, but if you're interested in one aspect, such as the battle of Red Bank, just go to the index at the rear and search for Red Bank or Winwick. If you find out anything else of interest, if you don't mind sticking a little post-it note on the page in question, that would be appreciated. In fact, you'll probably see there are several notes sticking out of most of these books already.'

'I can see that. Who needs an index? You've made the job a lot easier Jill.'

'Thank you. Before you go, sorry about yesterday when I had to leave you with the visitors from the States; how did it go?'

'It went very well. They were a lovely group, very knowledgeable. Janice did a great introduction on King Oswald, then we touched on the Titanic link and a bit on the Gerards, but it turned out they were a bit rushed for time as they were sailing out of Liverpool in the evening. One of the ladies gave me her card. She's in the tourism industry and is interested in promoting the church as a possible tourist destination.'

'That's really good news.'

'And they left a donation of fifty pounds.'

'Then that's double good news,' Jill replied with a beaming smile. 'I'm very grateful for all that Janice and you do for the church.'

'Well I know that Janice would agree with me when I say that the pleasure is all ours, so thank you Jill. Anyway, I'd better get back, as I've got some reading to do. Oh, just before I go ...' Alex pulled out a plastic bag with the pipe stems he had found. 'I went for a quick walk in Moors Field; this is what I found.'

'What are they?'

'Clay pipe stems, and I think they're old, possibly seventeenth century.'

'Yes, I can recognise them now. How interesting, and they were just sitting on the surface?'

'Yes, in the furrows.'

As Alex walked out of the rectory, he was feeling very happy. *Great result. Jill has loaned me some books, has agreed to a display in church and, most importantly, she's on my side.*

When he arrived home, Karen's car was on the drive. He wisely took off his boots and left them outside before entering the house. 'Only me,' he shouted.

'Hi,' was the reply, 'I'm in the lounge.'

Alex took his coat off and hung it up in the hall cupboard. He walked into the lounge. 'What have you been up to?' he asked, before kissing Karen on the cheek.

'You always make it sound like I've been up to no good.'

'Well have you?'

'I'll treat that comment with the contempt it deserves.'

She was sitting on the sofa reading a book entitled *The Colonisation of North America*. 'Did you know that the *Mayflower* was only one hundred feet long?'

'Of course.'

'Whatever,' Karen replied, smiling. 'A man came into the museum this morning with an impressive scale model of the *Mayflower* made from matchsticks and he wanted to know whether we were interested in buying it. He said it had taken him seven years to make. When I said that I was sorry, but I didn't think we were buying at the moment, he put it down on the table and said, "Well you can have it for free then, because I'm sick of the sight of it," and he left. He wouldn't sign any paperwork or give any details. He just left, so that's why I borrowed this book from the library and why I'm reading about the *Mayflower*.'

'Oh right,' said Alex, 'sorry I asked.'

'Don't be. It's really quite interesting. And what have you been up to?'

'Okay, well I told you about the conversation I had yesterday with Les Pritchard.' Karen nodded. 'I went to see him, and he gave me the documents from the

English Civil War Society, and he agreed to let me go on his land. So that's where I've been ... on his land.'

'Doing what?'

'Oh, I just went field walking to see if I could find anything of interest.'

'And did you?' Karen yawned her way through her question.

'Oh, sorry, am I keeping you awake?' Alex got up and walked out of the room, into the hall and recovered the clay pipe stems from his coat pocket. He walked back into the lounge and produced a small clear plastic bag, which contained the finds. He presented them to Karen by annoyingly thrusting the bag in front of her eyes. She snatched the bag and opened its contents on to the front cover of the book she was reading.

'So, the farmer is a smoker,' she said.

'Maybe. Or maybe they belonged to someone else.'

'Maybe they're the remnants of a seventeenth century barn dance,' Karen replied jokingly.

'Why do you say seventeenth century?'

'Well if you look at the stem size, I know for a fact that they're much bigger in diameter than the later pipes and yet the earlier versions had such small bowls. Really, this is at the time when smoking was starting to become popular, but tobacco was still expensive and in relatively short supply. In the eighteenth century the stems became long and thin but the bowls bigger. The idea was based around the concept of a long cool smoke. Finding a bowl would be a better indicator but I think mid to late seventeenth century would be a good educated guess, and I think you'll find that I'm correct.'

'Then I bow to your superior knowledge Mrs Helsby; except I don't, because I already knew that.'

Karen picked up a cushion and threw it at him, hitting him square in the face, which he ignored and continued. 'They look like Civil War era clay tobacco pipe stems, and seeing as it's a battlefield, you've just confirmed what I thought, they're soldiers' pipes.'

'So, what are you thinking of doing about it?'

'Well I want to do as little digging as possible. Les doesn't want me to dig any trenches, and my back isn't up to it anyway, so I'm going to dust down my metal detector, put some new batteries in it, and see how we go.'

'Not exactly the best time of the year for it.'

'On the contrary, young lady, it's nearly perfect. Bare soil, no growth, and damp ground, which enables a better signal.'

'So, when are you thinking of starting?'

'Tomorrow morning, depending on the weather. The only thing that will stop me is rain. Also, Jill has loaned me a couple of books and things about the Civil War. In fact, I'll just nip out to the car and get them.' Alex had walked to the front door and just opened it when he turned around and said, 'If we find anything, Jill has agreed that we can display it in church.'

Karen asked, 'What do you mean by we?' but Alex was on the drive and hadn't heard her, or pretended not to.

Alex spent the rest of the day reading about the battle of Red Bank and the day in question, 19 August 1648. Little did the Helsbys know what was in store. It could be famine or feast, and now was the time   to   find   out.

Chapter 5

Moors Field

THE FOLLOWING morning Alex pulled into Moors Field. As he passed through the hedgerow entrance, he could see the tyre tracks that he had left from the previous day, so knew that no vehicle had been in the field after him.

Privacy was his main concern. He didn't want to draw attention to himself, as it would only attract other people – other people with metal detectors and spades – and even without permission these types occasionally turn up, but usually after dark. They're called nighthawks, another word for thieves and trespassers who give metal detecting enthusiasts a bad name.

Alex's use of a metal detector was only occasional. He had bought the device about five years previously, after one of the archaeologists on a dig in Blackburn suggested it would be a good idea to start detecting on the spoil heap if they had a metal detector. Alex had always wanted one and this was the justification he needed.

Within the first hour of using his new toy, he had found a bronze servants bell, the type you see in the basement of a mansion house, usually connected to a kind of pull-cord mechanism in the living quarters or bedrooms. The site was actually the remains of a Victorian manor house, so the bell was completely in context with its surroundings, or it was until it was removed as part of a large clump of earth shovelled out of a lined concrete cistern in the basement. The cistern was apparently for irrigating the exotic fruits that were cultivated in the orangery.

Alex had only used the metal detector on a couple of other occasions since, because, as a rule, they were frowned upon by archaeologists and were not allowed anywhere near the trenches.

As he pulled into the field at 9.30 a.m., there was a very thin layer of fog sitting just above the ground. It was more or less static until a slight breeze took hold of it and drew it up the hill towards the copse. *This is spectacular. What a scene; everything feels right today.*

He parked the SUV just inside the hedgerow, parallel with the road, and jumped out. He opened the hatch and firstly changed his footwear to his walking boots, then retrieved some clear plastic bags in different sizes from his container box, which he called his toolbox, and stuffed them into his coat pocket. He then grabbed his trusty trowel, one which had been issued to him on his first dig. It should have been returned at the end of each day to the site container, but he had decided to keep it as it fitted well in his hand. He always planned to return it, maybe on the next dig.

Next out of the toolbox was a short spade, which was easy and light to carry. He grabbed half a dozen bamboo canes, each about a metre in height that he had cut from his garden the previous summer. *I think I'll mark a plot up near the treeline as a starting point.* His metal detector was next out and finally his Bronco hat, which he had bought in Australia two years ago. It was made of cowhide and it kept his head warm in winter and even warmer in summer. As a result, it was sweat stained around the forehead region.

He closed the hatch, locked the car and started walking towards the trees. Using the large tree on his right as a marker, he approached the centre of the field where he had left a mound of stones the previous day. *It should be about here.*

He looked around the immediate area, but the swirling fog was making it difficult. He decided to bend down as low as he could so he could see all the field beneath the fog. The little mound of stones was only about ten metres away. *This is really odd, the way that fog is hanging there above the ground.*

As he stood up again, he could only see the ground immediately around him. He started walking to where he thought the mound of stones was and within a few steps had walked into it, scattering the stones, like kicking a small pile of pebbles on the beach. He took one of his bamboo markers and twisted it into the soil beneath him. *A clay pipe marker; I'll get back to this later.*

As he continued walking towards the copse, he noticed that the breeze appeared to have changed direction. He could feel the cooling effect on his face, and the fog was now coming back down the hill towards him. He looked up and noticed that the blue sky was becoming milkier in colour. *Damn fog is closing in.*

He continued to walk in the direction that he last saw the trees. The ground was heavier now and started to stick to his boots again. *I'm not stopping until I get to the trees now that I'm here.* As he walked on, his back began to ache, then suddenly in front of him and reaching up high into the sky there were trees, big ones with large sticky buds, the next generation of leaves.

A few metres to his right he noticed what appeared to be a tree that had fallen recently and was revealing a huge root system, some of it partly submerged. The trunk itself was positioned at a nice height so he dropped all his equipment and sat down on the trunk, making sure that he pulled the back of his coat down to partly protect his denims from the dampness of the tree trunk.

His imagination suddenly began to work overtime as Royalist soldiers ran past him down the hill, running for their lives, screaming, 'Head for sanctuary at the church.' They were quickly followed by a group of Cromwell's Parliamentarian foot soldiers of the New Model Army. Shots were fired, screams could be heard, and the smell of black powder permeated the battlefield.

A good way down the hill a group of Royalists came across a farm cart in the field. They rolled it over and hunkered behind it, just desperate for some cover where they could load up and return fire with their matchlock muskets and pistols. The feeling of fear and absolute desperation was palpable as men fought hand to hand in a survival of the fittest.

Alex snapped out of his reverie when he heard what sounded like a shotgun being fired twice in an adjacent field. *Shotgun – I hope that was as far away as it sounded. Who would go shooting in the fog, even if they just got caught out by the weather? They shouldn't be firing their gun, surely.* He was slightly uncomfortable with his situation, knowing there was someone out there with a shotgun in the fog. *Just stay alert for someone approaching*, he told himself.

He pulled out a slightly damp piece of paper from his back pocket and opened it. It was a Google Earth map showing the fields on either side of Moorsdale Road, and he could see exactly where he was on the south side of the copse of trees. He pulled out his pen and drew a narrow rectangle in the field, travelling the full length of the trees. At full scale, the approximate length of the rectangle would be twenty-five metres by ten metres.

Alex, noticing that the fog was starting to lift, strode out the measurements and inserted a cane in each corner of the plot. He looked at the area marked out. *This is a good place to start. If soldiers were on the run in the direction of the church, they could hide or seek cover on the south side of these trees. By the same token, if they were seen they would come under fire. That's if there were trees here three hundred and sixty-nine years ago.* Alex pulled his mobile phone from his jacket pocket and called Karen.

'Hi love, are you still at home?'

'Yes,' she replied.

'Could you please do me a favour? Could you have a look at the tithe maps and ordnance survey online and see if you can see a copse or other depression in the centre of Moors Field.'

'Alex, I do this type of thing for a living and I don't want to be doing it on my morning off.'

'I know. I'm sorry, I forgot that you weren't in work this morning.'

'I'll take a quick look and call you back, but it will be quick.'

'You're a wonderful woman,' said Alex, but Karen ended the call before he had finished.

He came back to his base at the edge of the trees and sat on the tree trunk. The fog was now clearing quickly, and the sunshine was breaking through. He picked up his metal detector, turned it on and checked the battery display. A full battery was illuminated. He checked his settings and he was ready to go. *I'll start in the north-east corner, walk west, leave a one-metre gap, and then reciprocate the route.*

He walked to the north-east corner, put his headphones in place and headed west, with an attempt at a slow sweeping arc. Walking across the furrows it was slow progress and he was constantly adjusting the height of the coil by lengthening his arm to extend into each furrow.

Because he was constantly raising and lowering the coil head, it became virtually impossible to sweep at an arc; it was more of a pendulum swing in the valleys of the furrows, then on the ridges. He did his first length of the plot and was halfway back when he picked up a signal, which stayed strong as he pinpointed the exact spot. *The display is showing iron approximately four inches deep.* Alex marked the spot with the toe of his boot, put down his detector, removed his headphones and used his hand trowel on the black earth.

Within a minute he had revealed the source of the signal, a large iron industrial-type nut, and although it was corroding, he could see its internal thread and the fact that it was modern. *Probably off a tractor.* He picked up the nut and took it to the nearest bamboo plot stick and left it there. He expected that by the end of detecting this rectangular plot there may be quite a few finds deposited at the base of each bamboo plot marker, but only good finds would get bagged and pocketed.

He continued with his line back and forth until his mobile pinged with an incoming message tone – it was from Karen. He looked at the screen:

Checked all available maps re: your location, all show a copse of trees

Alex replied:

Thank you

He thought some more about his location. *If a copse of some sort was here during the Civil War, surely there must be evidence of the battle between the warring factions. Where else would you get cover from in an open field? You would expect the odd musket ball at least. Perhaps the evidence is too deep, or it's all been previously taken.*

He continued detecting until he came to the end of the plot. It was nearly lunchtime and he had six finds to show for a morning's work: two nuts, one bolt, one door hinge, one screw and one ball-valve mechanism from a water tank. He had collected the items, placed them in a carrier bag and was soon on his way back to the SUV for his packed lunch of a ham and tomato sandwich, a flask of coffee and a Kit Kat. *Now the fog has gone, it's warming up nicely; not bad for early March.*

Alex lifted the rear hatch and took his large black toolbox out of the SUV and placed it on the floor. He sat down in the boot with the hatch open and his legs dangling. His lunch was in a black elasticated string side pocket in the boot. He pulled his thermos flask out first and poured a steaming hot coffee into the lid, then extracted a sandwich from its aluminium foil wrapping. The exercise and fresh air had made him hungry so he made short work of his lunch, then lifted himself further into the boot so he could rest his feet. He opened the carrier bag containing his morning finds. *I'll take them home and bin them, then at least I'm getting the scrap metal out of his field.*

He decided to give Karen another call on her mobile. 'Hi, it's me.'

'Hi,' Karen replied. 'Have you found anything yet?'

'Oh yes, some lovely pieces of scrap metal. I've only done a small section of a huge field, so I'll be here for weeks, but the sun is shining now that the fog has cleared, so fingers crossed, you never know what's going to turn up. I've just had my lunch, so back to work in ten.'

'Break a leg.' Alex could tell that Karen was smiling as she said it. They said their goodbyes and finished the call.

Alex shuffled himself out of the rear of the car, bent down to put the toolbox in the back of the car and pulled the hatch closed. He felt that familiar twinge at the bottom of his back, but slightly to one side, and gave it a quick rub.

He began to walk up the field. *I can't see the canes.* Continuing his walk in the direction of the copse, he came across the single stick and small loose rocks, his previous marker. He could see all the other markers now. He marked out a new plot the same size but further south, away from the woods. Pulling the plan from his pocket, he marked his progress with a second rectangle alongside the first.

Having collected his equipment from his base at the tree trunk, he was now ready to get detecting. His device was working well and was indicating hits in excess of eight inches below the surface. He continued to find nuts and bolts in small amounts, but it was all ferrous, all iron-based, so he decided to make some adjustments to the settings on his metal detector.

The detector had the option to discriminate against certain metals, so he chose iron, and reset the device. Within minutes he had his first hit, which was a ring of brass with an internal thread. It was about the size of a golf ball, was obviously modern, and probably off a piece of farm machinery again. *Makes a change from rusty old iron.*

He continued back and forth across the furrows, feeling happy; he liked the outdoor life. When he had been working, he always yearned for the weekend when he could get out on a dig, or in the winter months to just get out and walk.

His continued pattern was taking him very slowly in a southward direction towards Winwick village. It was probably another hour before he had any further signals on his metal detector, then suddenly he had three all within a one-metre square. He moved the coil left and right and up and down to try to locate the first hit, but the hits must have been that close together that it was difficult to separate them. In the end he dug out an area of soil about two widths of the spade head square and about six inches in depth. The detector had indicated something at four inches deep.

He placed the excavated soil on the ground right next to the hole and started to sift through it, just using his hands and a trowel. The first find made a slight metallic ping as he touched it with his trowel. What he picked up was small and as he cleaned it between his fingers he could see that it looked like a brass button, about one inch in diameter with its edges curled under, a bit like an umbrella, except this would have let the rain in because it had two small holes in its centre, presumably to allow it to be stitched to a material. Alex slipped the button into a small plastic bag and then into one of his jacket pockets.

The second find came away from the soil in his hand and looked like a replica of the first. He bagged and pocketed the find. The third find he could see as soon as the soil fell away, due to the trowel's insertion. It was what looked like a belt buckle. He picked it up and cleaned it between his fingers. *This looks interesting, but I can't tell if it's old or modern. It looks like an older design; in fact, it looks like a military tunic belt buckle and the buttons reminded me of tunic buttons too.* He took a closer look to see if there were any identifying marks, but there was nothing he could see, so he bagged it up and put it in his jacket pocket. *I'll get my toothbrush on that when I get home.*

Alex continued detecting with renewed energy. He looked up for a second and noticed a pair of buzzards circling high above, powerful birds with huge wingspans, just gliding on the thermals. Against the clear blue sky, it was an impressive sight. Then just for a second his eyes were drawn to the entrance to the field, where he thought he saw movement in the hedgerow opening. *Probably a fox or rabbit.* All appeared still, so he continued his work.

It wasn't long before he came to the end of his second plot, and with no further finds he decided to call it a day. He gathered his equipment together and returned to the SUV, loading his equipment into the boot, then taking off his jacket and throwing it on to the passenger seat before jumping into the vehicle. He couldn't resist having a quick look through his jacket pockets at today's finds.

When he got home his daughter Louise was doing homework in her bedroom and Karen was out. 'Hi Lou,' he shouted.

'Hi Dad.'

'Where's Mum?'

'She's gone to the post office.'

'Okay,' Alex said as went into the kitchen and retrieved his finds from his jacket pocket and laid them out on the worktop in the utility room next to the sink. He opened the cupboard door beneath and retrieved the old toothbrush from a large glass. It was the odd-jobs glass, which also contained a screwdriver, a tube of superglue, a radiator vent key and some screws and Rawlplugs.

Rather than rinse each of his finds under the cold-water tap, he carefully brushed them with a wet toothbrush before allowing them to dry on a piece of kitchen tissue. For finer pieces he would use cocktail sticks or thorns to remove soil or debris.

An hour later Alex had showered and changed and made his way to the utility room to see how his finds had dried out. As he walked into the kitchen, Karen was just preparing tea. He walked up behind her, put his arms around her waist, and kissed her on the neck. 'I'm starving, what's for tea?' he asked. Karen pointed to the electric hob, where a large pan of pasta was bubbling away, the steam from the pan being extracted up through the cooker hood. Then she pointed at the adjacent pan, which had fried minced beef and what looked like a tomato-based sauce.

'It's called pasta bolognese,' she said. Alex opened his mouth to speak, then thought better of it. *I bet we've run out of spaghetti.*

He walked into the utility room and noticed his finds had gone. 'Karen, have you moved my finds?'

'Yes, have a look in the lounge.' Alex walked into the lounge, where on the coffee table sat one of his compartmental plastic display boxes, and he could see that each find was in its own section, sitting in its own little nest of acid-free paper. This paper was museum grade and was used to prevent any off-gassing, omitted as the by-product of a chemical process, such as corrosion.

'Thanks love, you didn't need to,' Alex shouted.

'I know. I'm just a wonderful wife.'

Alex and Karen spent some time that evening looking at his finds, using his new acquisition, an illuminating magnifying glass, which was basically a normal 90mm magnifying glass with a slightly deeper surround that contained several LEDs powered by batteries in the handle. Karen agreed with Alex that there was a possibility that the buttons and buckle were military, Civil War-era finds, but there was no detail on any of the items that made them identifiable.

'Are you going back there again tomorrow?' asked Karen.

'Well I was thinking I might give it a full day tomorrow and if I have any decent finds, I can drop them in at Liverpool museum on Thursday while I'm out with Derek and Thomas. This week it's a Thursday Club.'

'Oh, great, thanks for telling me. We were supposed to be out looking at new carpets and then going on for lunch.'

'So sorry, I forgot. I'll rearrange the Thursday Club and come out with you.'

'You will not. I don't want to be blamed for breaking up the brothers on their blessed Thursday.'

'Rightly so,' replied Alex bravely, before feeling the full force of the sofa scatter cushion hitting his face.

The following morning Alex arrived at Moors Field at approximately 9.15 a.m., the sky clear and the sun shining. *No sign of any fog or even mist; a beautiful day.* On his way through the hedgerow track he noticed another set of tyre marks alongside his own from yesterday. They stopped abruptly, then he could see footprints appear at what would have been either side of the vehicle. *Probably dog walkers; they just let their dogs run free in the field, usually at night or very early morning.*

Alex parked the SUV, unloaded his kit and headed for the copse. This time his plan had changed, and his new plot took in the area that previously yielded so many clay pipes. He measured out another rectangle in line with the other two plots and kept the dimensions the same, twenty-five metres wide and ten metres deep. The bamboo cane that marked the clay pipe finds was roughly centrally positioned.

He took the plan from his rear pocket and marked this third rectangle and the marker for the clay pipe finds, then went to his mobile phone and opened the application for 'English Grid Reference Finder', completed the instructions, and a grid reference number was displayed. He wrote this number down on the plan adjacent to the central marker, then went to the north-east corner and headed west using the same pendulum principle, a reciprocal route with a one-metre gap.

He was very slow and methodical, keeping to his lines and moving the detector coil across the furrows with accuracy and consistency. Within the first hour just a couple of nails and a screw had been recovered, so he stopped for a second and realised he was now very close to the central clay pipe marker.

He visually triangulated between himself, the copse and the large tree in the hedgerow perimeter. *Come on, there's got to be something here.* The detector began to bleep with a slightly higher tone than normal and was indicating zinc, only about two inches below the surface. He pinpointed the bleep, took his headphones off and put the detector down.

Using his trowel, he cut a small section about four inches square then started to remove the soil and place it next to the hole he was making. Again, there was that familiar noise of metal on metal as the trowel struck a gold-and-black AA battery, which he picked up and looked at closely. Its lot expiry date was 2021. He couldn't help but laugh. *I'm supposed to be finding things from the past not things that are still in date.* Alex placed the battery near one of the canes to be disposed of later.

Now back at the find point he quickly ran the detector over the small hole and soil he had disturbed. There was a sharp bleep, the same pitch as before but gone in a second. He looked at the display just in time to see it was showing zinc again, at a depth of eight inches plus. *Probably another stupid battery.*

Moving the detector coil slowly now, he searched for a signal. Nothing. Then just as he was pulling the detector away to resume his route there was another sharp bleep. He had a rough idea now of the location of the signal, so he laid down his earphones and detector and started to shovel out a six-inch square of soil.

Suddenly, he heard a voice. Someone was approaching from behind. A startled Alex turned around to see a man, probably in his thirties, wearing military camouflage fatigue trousers, wellington boots and a large woollen fisherman-type sweater. *I wonder who this is; maybe a farmer wanting to know why I'm in the field.*

The man came closer, and Alex, standing at six feet tall, noted he was a good three inches smaller than him but of stocky build.

'Hi, I'm Ian,' the man said with a local accent, as he thrust his hand forward.

Alex shook his hand. 'Alex. Can I help?'

'Oh, I was just passing and thought I saw a car through the hedgerow. I can see you're metal detecting; had any luck?'

This guy has got some nerve, thought Alex. 'No, and I'm sorry to be blunt, but who are you?' he asked the stranger.

'Ian Wright. I'm a metal detectorist, and I did this field a couple of years ago. You won't find anything here. You're wasting your time.'

Alex was annoyed at Ian's arrogance. 'You're not backwards at coming forwards, are you?'

'Just thought I'd do you a favour and let you know that I've been all over this field. Anything that was here, I found.'

'So, you're telling me I'm wasting my time then.'

'Pretty much.'

'So, what did you find?' asked Alex.

Ian hesitated. 'A few bits and pieces. I reckon this field has been done so many times in the past.'

'Oh, right, so can I see these bits and pieces on the national database?'

'I'm afraid not. There was nothing of great value anyway. Any good bits I sold on the internet. That's what I usually do, just to make a few bob.'

Selling finds on the internet and not even having them recorded was a crime in Alex's eyes. Anything identified as historical or made of a precious metal should be reported so that it can be correctly identified, photographed, and its weight, dimensions and where and how it was found recorded.

'That's where we differ,' said Alex. 'I'm not doing it for personal financial gain, I'm doing it because I love history and our heritage, and in particular I love that church.' Alex pointed at St Oswald's spire. 'And anything relating to the Civil War I can display in there.'

'Ah, the honest type, are we?'

'Yes, I am. And I don't have trouble sleeping at night.'

'Nor I,' was the reply.

'Okay. Well I have permission to be in this field so if you don't mind, I'm going to carry on with what I was doing before you decided to come here and do me a favour,' said Alex, slightly annoyed.

'Okay. I'd like to say it's been a pleasure,' said Ian, turning away before he finished his sentence and walking towards a black vehicle parked near the hedgerow track.

Alex watched him go. *Looks similar to my Land Cruiser; just a bit too far away to see. What was wrong with that guy, or was it me being too sensitive? I never speak to people like that, but he made me feel angry. Did I overreact?*

Alex watched Ian all the way back to his car until he turned it around to exit the field. *Maybe that guy was right; it may just be the odd button or nail or battery that's left, or maybe he's just trying to scare me away so he can come back when it's dark to do some nighthawking. I'm just going to crack on and be more mentally prepared in case someone else decides to come and do me a favour.*

Alex went back to the hole that he had started to dig and took about four inches out with his spade, but because the earth was so soft, he decided to trowel the rest out, carefully sifting each tiny load through his fingers. He had gone to a depth of about ten inches without any success, so gave the hole a quick sweep with the detector. Nothing. He quickly swept over the spoil mound that he had created. Still nothing. He spread the mound out to a flat layer of soil and swept over it again with the detector. *Must have been a phantom signal. I still don't understand why that happens. Maybe it's the detector at fault.*

He was about to fill the hole in when a large earthworm burst through the soil, its skin glistening in the bright sunshine. Alex bent down to take a closer look and noticed several small pieces of clay pipe, the colour of soil. He picked a piece up and gave it a quick wipe on his sleeve to reveal the telltale off-white colour of the clay. He collected the pieces and put them in his pocket. *At least I'll have something to look at when I get home.* He backfilled the hole he had made and continued to sweep at a slow pace.

By late morning the weather had changed from blue sky to grey threatening cloud. Alex was just passing the clay pipe cane marker from the other day when his detector bleeped weakly and indicated a find approximately four inches below the surface. He pinpointed the signal and used his trowel to make a small hole, noticing that the soil seemed to be changing with each little excavation and this time there seemed to be a lot of pea-sized gravel in the soil.

He went through the same procedure of sifting each trowel-full through his fingers. *That felt different; looks like a small stone.* He wiped it between his fingers then rubbed it on his sleeve, removing the mud. *Yes, a lead musket ball,* thought Alex as he broke into a smile. It was only about one centimetre in diameter, but it had a good weight and that familiar patina that covers lead after a period of time. On its surface there was a slight flat spot, which could indicate it had been fired and maybe struck something hard. *My first-ever musket ball find.*

'Yes!' Alex said out loud. He slipped his find into a small plastic bag and wrote on it the grid reference number, copied from the plan he was carrying in his back pocket. He then placed the find in his pocket, rechecking the hole and spoil for any other signals before backfilling.

He was about to continue detecting with renewed enthusiasm, hope and excitement when suddenly the heavens opened. *I don't believe this; it looks like I'll have to call it a day.* He had been so preoccupied that he had taken his eye off the weather. The sky had darkened in all directions, so he gathered all his things as quickly as he could and headed back towards his SUV.

He noticed the temperature falling and before he knew it, he was being pelted by hailstones.

Fortunately, his Bronco hat afforded good protection until it got too wet, then it took on the appearance of wet chamois leather on his head. He headed back to the SUV as fast as he could, considering what he was carrying. The hail changed to even heavier rain and the mud stuck to his boots even more, every step he took sounding like a suction pad was attached to the underside of each boot.

After what felt like a lifetime, he eventually reached the SUV and opened the hatch, throwing all his equipment into the back, removing his jacket and throwing that in as well, then changing footwear. He slipped on a pair of old casual shoes, then banged the boots together to remove the surplus mud before placing them on a large black bin bag next to the toolbox. He closed the hatch and climbed in the vehicle at the driver's side.

All of a sudden, he felt water running down his back and realised he had forgotten to take off his Bronco hat, so he took hold of the rim and threw it like a Frisbee towards the toolbox in the rear, and as it spun it machine-gunned a series of water droplets across the inside of both near and passenger side windows.

As he turned the key and started the engine, the windows misted up straight away due to all the moisture on his clothing and equipment. He turned the fan to demist and decided to open the front passenger window just a couple of inches to help the process. Suddenly, and totally unexpectedly, there was a loud boom as a huge clap of thunder resonated through the air. Alex noticed that the partially open window rattled for just a second, before a huge fork of lightning came down and hit the trees in the copse. Within a matter of seconds one of the largest trees started to tumble. *That was a huge strike; it looks as if it's cut the tree right down the middle.*

As the tree fell it made that creaking noise of wood splitting under pressure, then a loud crack as the wood over-extended before crashing down into the field right where Alex had been detecting. *I'm so lucky I left when I did.*

There was another clap of thunder, even louder this time. Alex's eyes were fixed on the copse, not expecting lightning to strike twice in the same place. Then just a couple of seconds later a huge flash and another fork of lightning came down and hit another large tree on the edge of the copse. This time there was a crackling noise, then, just for a second, a puff of blue smoke and another tree or two were hit. They fell down, seemingly without complaint.

All three had fallen in parallel, away from the copse and into the field where Alex had been just a short while ago. Branches had splintered as the trees hit the ground and the lovely furrowed field looked as if a tornado had just passed through. *What an absolute mess. I must call Les.*

When he did, Les wasn't too pleased to found out about the damage the lightning had done and, through previous experience, he suspected there may be more damage in the copse, so he said he may even have to bring a few trees down himself. He instructed Alex to stay off the field but was absolutely delighted when he heard about the musket ball.

When Alex arrived home, he couldn't wait to tell Karen about the find of the day. 'Karen, come and see this,' he said as he pulled the small plastic bag from his pocket, opened it and placed the musket ball in her open hand. She looked at it closely then rolled it between her fingers.

'We've got some of these on display in the museum, but looking at this and feeling its weight and knowing that you found it on a battlefield site, it's really special. Well done,' she said with a smile, then kissed Alex on the cheek.

That evening Alex was sitting at the dining table having his evening meal with Karen. Louise had taken hers to her bedroom. 'I was having a great day until the weather changed. Oh, I forgot to tell you, some wise guy walked up to me and told me I was wasting my time because basically he had taken anything worth taking and sold his finds on the internet.'

'So, what did you say?' asked Karen.

'Well, I lost my temper a bit and told him that I don't have any problem sleeping at night, and do you know what he said? "Nor do I." He doesn't report his finds. He probably doesn't even report it to the landowner. He just sells them on for profit. I bet he never even gets permission to go on other people's land.' Alex was raising his voice.

'Calm down Alex, for goodness sake. It's a hobby; you're doing it for pleasure.'

'I know,' said Alex in a calmer voice. 'I just don't like people who take the ...'

'Okay, I know what you mean,' Karen interrupted, 'but I've been doing a little research myself,' she said teasingly. Alex looked up at her.

'Ah, I have your interest now I see,' she added. Alex forced a smile. He knew only too well that when his wife was interested, whatever she had to say would be worth listening to. Karen continued,

'Remember when you asked me to look at the maps to see if I could see a copse on Moors Field?' Alex nodded. 'Well I've been looking at those maps again. It was mainly the field layout that caught my attention.'

She picked up a map from the sofa. 'This old tithe map covering Winwick is dated 1846. There are no road names, just landmarks, field boundaries etc. You can see Moors Field and you can see the copse; however, if you travel south in the direction of St Oswald's Church, you'll notice that there are no boundaries or fences shown on this map. It appears that it used to be one huge piece of land for growing whatever, from the copse all the way to Claybarn Field, only one hundred metres short of the church.

'For a battlefield there really was nowhere to hide. This was a farmer's huge field. If you were running down the hill away from the copse in Moors Field you would eventually come to the valley bottom, then you would start going up the incline towards Claybarn Field and the church. You're a sitting duck. Also, something else … I found out that on 19 August 1648, the weather was torrential rain. It had rained for days; the brooks were overflowing, and the fields were flooded. It was a particularly bad summer.'

'It doesn't bear thinking about,' Alex said. 'It must have been sheer hell just trying to walk, never mind run and fight. Thanks for this, I can see you spent some time on it.'

'I haven't finished yet. This is the best bit. I want you to look at this drone footage I've just found, again on the internet, somebody doing it for fun.' Karen took hold of her tablet and stood it in its stand on the kitchen table, then played the footage of a bird's-eye view of the steeple of St Oswald's Church. The drone seemed to circle it a couple of times before it ascended to give an overall view of the church and how it stood in its surroundings. Suddenly she froze the shot, and Alex could see it was a perfect view over Claybarn Field to the copse in Moors Field.

'Just watch this,' she said. 'I'm just going to zoom in slowly to Claybarn Field.'

'Wait. In this corner of the field,' Alex said, pointing at the screen, 'that would be the south-east corner, and the nearest point to the church. Does that look like some sort of earthworks?' He was pointing at an area in the corner of the field that was tucked away near to the stone perimeter wall, with a small area of shrubbery around the wall on the edge of the field.

'It does,' said Karen, 'but this was filmed in the summer when the fields were full of pre-harvest crops. It could be a wind anomaly that has levelled the crops at that location.'

'What we need is a winter shot,' said Alex.

'Okay, I'll look on Google Earth.' Karen picked up the tablet and entered the location, then slowly zoomed in to the corner of the field. This time it was a winter shot, there were no crops on show, just dark soil, but the furrowing highlighted slight depressions in the soil at that location.

'There is or was definitely something there or created there,' said Karen. 'There are no other depressions in the field at all, and the fact that it's an L-shaped structure means it was probably man-made.'

Alex was studying the screen intensely. 'I think I've seen something like this before at a similar location, at the start of a road that runs through open field. I think it could be evidence of a turnpike. I know this road historically was a turnpike, and this would be a logical place to put a toll collection point. It was basically a shelter that would usually have been of wood, stone or brick at which the attendants would charge people requiring passage through a gate or barrier. It could date back to as early as the sixteenth century or as late as the nineteenth century.'

'So, what's your next step Alex?'

'Well I have to stay off Moors Field because the storm brought down a couple of trees. You should have seen the fork lightning. It was so close that I could feel the static in the air. Anyway, there will be tractors and all sorts in there tomorrow as they'll have to cut and remove the fallen trees. I'm out with the boys tomorrow at Thursday Club, so on Friday I'll look at making a start on Claybarn Field.'

'Well remember to stay away from any trees, particularly in a storm. Don't stand under them for shelter like some people do.'

'Oh, I didn't know you cared,' replied Alex sarcastically.

'I don't. I was just thinking about the poor dog walker who would happen to come across your corpse,' Karen said, walking away.

'Right, that's it,' shouted Alex, as he chased her into the kitchen.

Karen squealed, 'I didn't mean it. I didn't mean it.'

Chapter 6

Claybarn Field

ALEX ENJOYED his day out with his brothers; they ended up going rifle shooting at an outdoor activities club in Delamere Forest then drove to Liverpool, dropped the finds off at the museum for identification and recording, and called in for a late lunch in a bar/restaurant in the Albert Dock area of the city.

Alex told Derek and Thomas about his metal detecting exploits and they both offered their services, knowing full well that Alex liked to work alone.

'The offer is there if you need us,' said Thomas, as Derek nodded his approval.

The following day, Friday, had always been Alex's favourite day of the week. It was that end-of-week feeling that most Monday to Friday workers had, and it got better as the day went on. He still enjoyed it, even in retirement. Louise was also well aware of her father's mood on a Friday and very rarely missed the opportunity to ask for the money to buy a new outfit or similar for the weekend. Alex knew the game she was playing and often strung her along for hours before giving in. On occasions he just said no.

After breakfast with Karen and Louise, on one of his 'no' days, he was ready and loaded for more metal detecting, but this time in Claybarn Field. He had discussed this with Karen the previous night and decided not to be distracted by the possibility of the turnpike refuge at the top of the field. It would have to wait until he had finished because it would involve serious digging.

Alex left home in his beloved SUV. The sun was shining but you could still see your breath in the cold air. As he approached Winwick he decided to drive past Claybarn Field and headed for Moors Field. As he pulled through the gap in the hedgerow, he noticed the track was now seriously rutted, and when he looked to his right in the direction of the copse, it was a scene of devastation. Numerous large-wheeled tractors had driven up the field with a large flatbed truck and ripped the earth to pieces, leaving a series of deep gouges and huge troughs the full length of the field.

At the copse there were two men with circular saws cutting the fallen trees into manageable logs. There was a plume of blue smoke mixed with sawdust, which lingered around them as the saws competed for the loudest buzz. *Crying shame for the trees and the field, and the fact that I must move on. I'll come back next year maybe, but for now it's Claybarn.*

Alex turned the SUV in a full 360-degree circle and nearly became stuck in the mud as he slowed, but just had enough revs to pull him through to Moorsdale Lane. The tyres threw mud and stones into the wheel arches and then into the air as they made purchase on the road surface. As he turned right, he looked in his rear-view mirror to see that he had left a trail of muddy tyre tracks on the road behind him.

As the stones continued to spit from the wheels into the wheel arches, it sounded like someone was shooting airgun pellets at his car. After about a hundred metres the noise stopped, and the tracks dried up as everything was finally expelled from his treads. Just a short distance down Moorsdale Lane he pulled through the hedgerow into Claybarn Field and was delighted to see that the track was in decent condition.

He turned right and drove down to the bottom of the field on a narrow trackway. *The ground is very flat here, a bit like a shallow valley bottom*. He pulled up and started to remove his equipment from the SUV.

He looked up the incline in the direction of the church, which was just off to the left, and noticed that the system of furrows didn't seem as deep as Moors Field, but the soil looked lighter in colour and not as wet. *I think I'll go field walking before I put my markers down.*

He set off up the incline, but after only two or three steps he noticed a claggy soil stuck to his boots. *That's an unpleasant surprise. I thought this was going to consist of more sand than anything going by its colour, but it's laden with clay.* He continued walking up the hill and before he knew it, he was right at the location that he had pinpointed on Google Earth the previous day, which showed undulations in the earth. *I can't see anything that's obvious. The ground looks perfectly level, maybe it's the result of ploughing.*

He investigated that corner of the field for a good fifteen minutes and the only things of note were fragments of clay tobacco pipes. *Clay pipes in a field of clay.* Alex shook his head and smiled to himself. *I must be mad, but I love it — exercise, fresh air, no hassle and being where I want to be, the great outdoors.*

Continuing his walk up and down Claybarn Field he found nothing of any substance. Undeterred, he walked back to the SUV and poured himself a coffee from the thermos flask. From the inside pocket of his coat, he pulled out an overhead photograph of the field and drew the equivalent of a twenty-five metre by ten metre rectangle at the northernmost boundary of the field on the photograph. *I'll detect up the hill in plots, the same as before, heading towards the boundary hedge and then come back down. I reckon about ten runs should cover the main area of this field that I'm interested in.*

He finished his coffee and slid the photograph back inside his jacket pocket. He picked up his Bronco hat, which had gone stiff from the soaking it had received the other day, and placed it on his head. With his detector, small shovel, trowel, a pocket full of plastic bags, and four cane markers under his arm, he set off to mark out the first plot.

He was now getting used to walking with the extra weight in the form of clay adhering to his boots, occasionally stopping to strike each boot with the shovel in the hope of expelling as much muddy clay as possible and easing the stress on his calves, which helped his back. As always, Alex set off with the best intentions and high levels of enthusiasm. He was using his same pendulum method as in Moors Field due to the furrowing, but there were large areas where the furrowing was so shallow that he could return to the sweeping arc method.

After some very early hits on or near the surface, consisting of the usual nuts, bolts, screws and nails, he decided to discriminate against iron-based or ferrous metals by adjusting the settings on his metal detector. He had no further hits in that section, so he moved the cane markers to the next plot and marked it on the photograph.

As he slowly swept up the hill, once again he drifted away, and his imagination got the better of him. He was in the middle of the battle of Red Bank, but from the safety of an overhead perspective, as a group of Scottish Royalists were running up the hill, dishevelled, exhausted and soaking wet due to the constant rainfall. They turned and reloaded before firing their muskets at the oncoming Parliamentarians of Cromwell's New Model Army. Again, they turned and ran up the hill at an extremely slow pace, stumbling in the mud, panicking, running for their lives, and a cry of 'sanctuary in the church' could be heard above the shouts of pain and anguish. The sound of black powder exploding its fiery lead from the muzzle of a Parliamentarian musket was all around.

Suddenly he was disturbed from his reverie by the bleep of his detector through his headphones. He pinpointed the spot, showing six inches deep on the display, so he used his small spade to cut a square out of the soil. He lifted a section out in one piece and, as he lay it on its side, he could clearly see that only the top three inches were soil and the rest consisted of dense clay. He started to break the clay up carefully using his trowel like a knife to force it open. *That looks interesting. Looks like a small piece of black leather.* He released the leather from the grip of the clay and immediately noticed it was a very small drawstring purse and its weight indicated that there was something inside.

Alex opened the pouch carefully by inserting his index finger in the top to release the drawstring. When he had opened it sufficiently, he turned the bag upside down and emptied the contents into his left hand. *It's not gold but I'm so lucky to find these.* Displayed in the palm of his left hand were two Charles I pennies, both dated 1642, and a silver Charles I half crown dated 1643.

They weren't in mint condition; they were well worn but you could still see all the detail. The pennies showed a bust of Charles from the side wearing a crown and ruff collar, and on the rear of the coin was a heraldic-type shield. The half crown showed Charles on horseback with his sword in the air, and on the reverse was again a heraldic-type shield. The coins were a lovely find and they were so clean after living in a small leather purse for over three hundred and fifty years.

Alex was smiling as his gaze was transfixed by the coins, then he looked at the leather pouch, which was still in his other hand. He was feeling it between his fingers. *It may be dirty, but the quality and the texture of the leather, it could have been made yesterday. Something that old shouldn't look this good.*

Then he recalled a similar situation only a couple of years ago. At the time he was a volunteer on the dig at the Roman fort Vindolanda near Hadrian's Wall. For one day he had the privilege of working at the coalface, so to speak, which was a section of the dig where lots of finds and artefacts had been recovered in an absolutely amazing condition of preservation because they were in an anaerobic layer.

At Vindolanda the anaerobic layer was created in the domestic environment by the laying of new clay floors on to old, and trapped between them was straw used as carpet, and anything else that was dropped into the carpet on a regular basis, such as toys, combs, shoes and coins. An item that's trapped within an anaerobic layer is without any air or oxygen, so it doesn't decay at the normal rate, in fact in perfect conditions, not at all. At Vindolanda the numbers of textiles, leather goods and world-famous writings on tablets and parchments that were being recovered in this preserved condition were spectacular.

Alex carefully placed each coin in its own little bag before placing them in his pocket. Then he took out his mobile phone and went to the grid reference application. Once he had received the number, he wrote it down on the photograph, then wrote it down on a cane marker, which he twisted into the ground adjacent to the hole. For good measure he then wrote down the grid reference number and date on each coin bag. He then bagged the leather pouch and did the same. *This clay may be awful to dig and work in, but the potential finds in this field are beyond imagination.*

Alex's eyes were drawn to the entrance through the hedgerow. *It's difficult to tell from here but it looks like someone standing there, very still.* Then there was a flash of very bright light, like the sun reflecting off a mirror, glass or something metallic. There was a glint just for a second, then it was gone, then it was there again. *I'm going to walk over there to see who it is.*

As soon as Alex began to walk in the direction of the light, he could see someone turn around and leave, so he stopped, thinking it pointless now that the person had scarpered. However, he felt uneasy at the thought of somebody watching what he was doing, or even worse, watching what he was finding. Not that they would be able to see much, as it was too far away.

Alex got back to the job in hand and swept the area of the find before levelling it. *If there's an anaerobic layer it could preserve almost anything; I think I'll switch back to detecting all metals.* He stopped, adjusted the settings on his detector, and glimpsed over towards the field entrance, but struggled to see anything in the distance. *I don't believe it. The fog is coming back again. We've had our fair share of foggy days already this spring.*

Despite this, he continued detecting, and sure enough, within thirty minutes he had found a lovely example of a twenty-first century nut and bolt, complete with spring washer. *Just what I always wanted.*

The fog descended suddenly, like a thick heavy blanket, subduing any traffic noise. The birds seemed to stop singing, and the air was heavy and damp. *I need to make my way back to the SUV, but I've lost my bearings. I can't see a treeline; in fact, I can't see anything.* He picked up his spade and detector and started to walk.

More by luck than judgement he made it back to the SUV, having realised that the satnav application on his mobile was no use in the middle of an empty field. He loaded his equipment into the rear of the vehicle, picked up his carrier bag of sandwiches and his thermos flask and sat in the driver's seat. *I'll give it half an hour see if the fog starts to clear again.*

He turned on the radio and decided to take the morning's finds out of his pocket. Suddenly there was a loud bang on the roof. Alex jumped out immediately, breathing deeply as he looked on the roof, then ran around the car for any evidence of the cause. On the floor near the passenger door was a piece of wood, like a piece of cut timber, the type you buy in the DIY stores to burn on the patio heater or log burner. He looked on the roof of the SUV, more carefully this time, and could see some remnants of wood bark sitting in quite a substantial indentation. *I don't believe this, somebody must have thrown that log, unless they're falling off trees pre-cut these days.*

'Who's there? shouted Alex. 'Show yourself.' He stood perfectly still … waiting, listening. The fog was swirling around him, and he could barely see his outstretched hand in front of him. He felt vulnerable and very exposed. *I'm heading home.* He jumped into the SUV, fired up the engine and turned on the headlights, which had very little impact as the fog just reflected the light, so he turned them down to just the side lights and made his way slowly up the field towards the exit.

As he turned to exit the field through the hedgerow he braked suddenly. *Someone just walked in front of the car.* Then there was more movement to the side – two, maybe three people, brushing past in a fraction of a second. *This doesn't feel right. I'm off.* He edged his way down the track and accelerated on to Moorsdale Lane, totally unable to see any traffic approaching from either direction. He just needed to get out of that field.

Later that same afternoon he decided to call his brothers, just to explain what had happened. They were delighted with his finds, but they were both of the same opinion, that someone was trying to frighten him off the field. When Alex explained about his meeting with the suspected nighthawk Ian, they both agreed that there was a good chance that he was the culprit. Derek and Thomas offered help in the form of support in the field, but Alex said he was alright and didn't intend to find himself in that situation again.

That evening Alex had a long discussion with Karen about the day's events. She too was delighted and fascinated by the coins and pouch find but was concerned about his safety.

The weekend was a total disaster weather-wise; fog and dense fog was the order of the day all weekend. Alex went to church on Sunday morning, which gave him the opportunity to update Les and anyone else who was interested in his progress. On Sunday afternoon he had emailed the finds liaison officer with a description and photographs of his latest coin finds, and he was asked to take them to the museum.

The start of a new week brought fine clear crisp weather. Alex made his way to Claybarn Field, optimistic that he would find more and better finds, but he was still very concerned that someone was paying interest in his activities and was trying to warn him off. But this made him more stubborn than ever, knowing that someone else wanted what he was currently looking for.

He looked up at the roof inside the SUV, where there was no trace of the thump that he had given it when he arrived home on Friday, which resulted in the indent in the roof from the log incident springing out and disappearing. *Who needs a body shop?*

When he arrived at the entrance to the field, he turned left up the trackway towards the high end of the field nearing the church. He gathered his things from the SUV and walked into the field, and as he approached, he began to see that his cane markers were still in place. On Friday he had been unable to see them, or anything else for that matter.

As he got closer, he noticed numerous mounds of earth scattered in the area. He approached one and was shocked at what he found – a hole about thirty centimetres square and forty-five centimetres deep had been dug. He went to the next mound and found the same. Within his twenty-five metre by ten metre plot he counted twenty-eight holes that had been dug, some larger than others, some even made into small trenches. It was devastating.

Alex called Les, informing him that someone had been in his field digging rather large holes and it wasn't him. Les didn't seem too upset but he was on his way to have a look to see what the damage was. Meanwhile, Alex took a walk around the plot and noted that there were no holes outside of the marked area. *Why would they stay within my area when they could go anywhere in this field? Is it because they saw what I had found through binoculars and wanted to stay in that location, knowing it was rich? Or were they planning to use my system of operating in plots, so they were never going over old ground? But why would they want to go over ground that I've already detected? Do they have a better specification metal detector? One that goes deeper, probably, especially looking at the depth of holes they've dug.*

In one of the holes Alex spotted what looked like a small piece of paper that had been screwed up and tossed away, so he bent down and picked it up. *It's just a sweet wrapper.* He then noticed a large tractor coming up the trackway. It veered off and headed in his direction, the huge wheels ploughing through the earth with consummate ease but maximum damage as far as Alex was concerned. *What the hell!*

Alex waved at the driver to stop, which he did, but not before the tractor approached the perimeter of the plot. Les jumped out of the cab, wearing blue overalls, and wellington boots. His large frame approached. 'Sorry Les, I just thought you were going to drive straight into this area, which I haven't finished yet.'

'Looks like someone has already finished it for you,' Les replied. The men shook hands fondly. 'What's been going on Alex?'

'I'll show you.' They only had to walk a couple of metres to come across one of the holes.

'When do you think this happened?' asked Les.

'Could be any time since Friday afternoon. I finished early because of the fog, and a couple of strange things happened. I thought I was being watched. I swear I drove past people on the way out of the field, but it was so difficult to see, as the fog was as dense as I've ever experienced. But there were definitely people here, and someone threw a log that landed on my roof; it was pre-cut, not a branch falling from a tree.'

'That's not good,' said Les, concerned. 'If you want to give it up, I fully understand. That sounds like quite a frightening experience.'

'It was, but I don't want to give it up so someone else can come in and strip the fields bare for a fast buck. Anything found here should be recorded for historical reasons.'

Les agreed. 'I know. You're preaching to the converted, but it's been a problem for many years.

These fields aren't gated, and that wouldn't stop people coming in anyway.'

'They're trying to frighten me off Les.'

'I'm afraid that's what it looks like.'

They carried on looking at a few of the other holes. 'These larger ones could cause us a few problems. I can get a small digger in to backfill them,' said Les.

'That won't be necessary, I'll do it by hand. You've given me access to your field, so it's the least I can do.' *I think I may regret that offer.*

'You're a good man Alex. And I have an idea. I have a couple of old Land Rovers at the farm, so I think I'll drive one around and park it up where your car is now, and just leave it there for the duration, just so it looks like someone is in the field. I'm not sure it will stop them at night mind, but you never know.'

'I don't want to put you to any trouble.'

'The only trouble I'll be in is if the police stop me driving it here, as it's not taxed or insured.' They shook hands again, then Les returned to the tractor and reversed over his old tracks before turning the vehicle to exit through the hedgerow.

Oh well, I'll make a start on filling these holes, thought Alex. *Actually no; I think I'll sweep over these spoil heaps, just in case our friends have done me a favour and left me a morsel.*

When he approached the largest spoil heap, he spread it out with his spade first before sweeping it with his detector. He heard that familiar noise, metal on metal and knelt down for a closer look.

In a slice of clay, he could see a Y-shaped piece of iron. He cleaned the clay away and held the piece of iron in his hand. *I know what that is, it's a musket rifle stand. They have one in Karen's museum.* These rifle stands were used extensively in the Civil War; they were attached to a pole, which was dug into the ground. The long barrel of the musket could then be rested in the Y shape to offer support whilst the musketeer fired. *Looks about fifteen centimetres long. The pole would have been splintered by ploughing and rotted away. A lovely find though.* He bagged the find, obtained the grid reference number from the mobile application, and wrote the number on the bag and the photograph.

Alex was happy. It was something new and pertinent to the English Civil War. *If the nighthawks leave items like this behind, I wonder what they've taken away. Maybe it's a sign that they were discriminating against iron and only looking for the valuables, which sounds about right, and it sounds a bit like it could be Ian.*

Alex went to all the other spoil heaps, but he had no further finds. He then proceeded to backfill all the holes, which seemed to take an age, before walking back to the SUV for a coffee from his thermos flask.

Sitting in the rear with his legs dangling, he looked out across the field. Although he felt his work had been violated, he knew that he had to box clever. Then his phone pinged with the familiar noise of an incoming email. It was from the finds liaison officer confirming the authenticity of the musket ball.

A lead musket or pistol ball, with an uneven appearance, and two distinct nodules on the line of moulding/casting. One large indentation from either firing or plough action in the soil. Broad period post-Medieval circa AD 1600 to AD 1700.

The other items, such as the buttons and belt buckle, were all confirmed as being post-Medieval, of military design, and estimated to date from circa AD 1600 to AD 1750. The email went on to say he could collect the items when he was taking any other finds in for authenticity identification. *Fantastic, this is as good a confirmation as you can get. I'm going to get a small cabinet made to display these items in the historical section of the church.* Alex felt really satisfied with this report, as it validated everything that he was doing and the amount of time he was committing to this venture.

He pulled the photograph from one of his many jacket pockets and looked at how he was progressing. The rectangles had been drawn on to the photograph and were now forming a grid pattern as they did in Moors Field. The obvious thing to do now was to carry on up the hill in a new plot. He looked at the photograph then at the field. *I've got plenty of cane markers, so I'm going to plot out some decoy markers well away from my detection area.*

Alex was looking at an area far over on the western side of the field about a hundred metres away. *Can't go too far over or they won't see the markers from the trackway. I'll have to disturb the ground over there in a few places, make it look as if I'm on to something, or at least searching for something.*

He was distracted by an old Land Rover crawling up the hill towards him; it was blowing out more blue smoke than the circular saws at Moors Field last week. Green and cream in colour, it looked as if it had been parked under a tree of nesting birds for the last twenty years. Slowly it approached, until Alex could see it was Les driving.

Further down the field, a tractor was following Les, presumably to take him back to where he was going after delivering the Land Rover. Les veered around Alex's SUV at the last minute, turned the Land Rover around and came to a halt near to the top of the hill and the field perimeter. He walked down the hill towards Alex.

'She's available for hire, for weddings and funerals,' Les said in a jovial manner.

'I'll bear that in mind,' replied Alex.

Les continued on his way. 'Got to shoot mate, sorry,' he shouted as he approached the tractor. Alex gave him a wave as the tractor turned to leave; Les stuck his arm out of the cab window as they left.

Alex returned to his thoughts. *I can't really do a lot more to keep these guys away. Just try my best and give myself a chance to get some nice finds.* He grabbed a pile of cane markers from the toolbox and headed across the field to set up the decoy plot. Once the markers were in place, he made sure there was a clear and unobstructed view from the field entrance. At each marker point he inserted two canes, which stood out clearly as markers.

Before he left the plot, he dug a couple of small holes, left some small piles of earth, and generally just kicked things around to make it look as if that was where he was detecting. He walked back to his current plot and, as he removed each cane, he left a small pile of stones. He then started another plot immediately next to his current one and marked it with small stones in each corner. He then penned the new plot to the grid on the photograph and commenced detecting.

He hadn't received a signal in quite a while and the doubt started to set in. *I wonder if the machine is working correctly. Not a screw or nail. Maybe the batteries are low.* Then the telltale bleep of a ferrous hit, the meter informing him it was over eight inches in depth.

Once he had pinpointed the find, he dug out a section of mainly clay about a foot square and carefully sliced through it with his trowel. To his surprise he slowly revealed an iron stirrup, which still had a small piece of leather strap attached. It was in an amazing condition, and the design suggested it was old. *Beautiful. What a find. I'm so lucky. This could be a Cavalier stirrup or a Parliamentarian horseman stirrup from the Civil War. I'm betting it's of that age.* Alex felt like jumping for joy but settled for a more reserved fist pump and a quiet 'yes'. He bagged his find, labelled it, got the grid reference from the app, then wrote it on his photo grid.

Throughout the remainder of the morning Alex moved on, working up the hill, replotting on his photo grid, and before lunch he had successfully retrieved four lead musket balls, three of which were together in the same hole. This was his best haul to date and, as he sat in the back of the SUV eating his lunch, he was looking forward to the day when his finds could be proudly displayed in St Oswald's Church.

The Y-shaped support, the stirrup and the four musket balls were laid out on a sheet of newspaper for another look before they were returned to their individual bags. Alex perused the photo grid, looking at his advancement up the hill and the location of each find marked in his trail. *Definitely more finds on this incline. Perhaps the soldiers fell in the mud and dropped items from their clothing, or maybe they were shot as they tired, due to the hill and conditions. Or they could have turned and fought a fighting retreat, bringing down a horseman and sending him to an early grave.*

He tidied up in the rear of the SUV and decided to have a look at the old Land Rover, which was parked about ten metres away behind him. Its appearance didn't improve as he approached it. The vehicle was absolutely caked in bird droppings, and there was even moss attached to the front nearside wing panel. Through the front window Alex could see caging that separated the cabin from the rest of the vehicle, and it looked like it contained hay or straw. He went around the back and looked through the window and confirmed that that was the case; it was jam-packed with square bales of hay. *A rodent's paradise*, he thought.

As he walked back to the SUV, he pulled out his photo grid and looked at the L-shaped structure in the corner of the field that Karen had previously pointed out, and realised it was positioned in line with a lamp post situated on the other side of the hedgerow. He turned back and walked towards the Land Rover but keeping the lamp post in his eyeline. He stopped next to the vehicle, suddenly conscious of exactly where he was standing, in line with the lamp post. Studying the photo grid, he realised that, according to his calculations, the Land Rover was parked right next to the L-shaped structure, if not directly on top of it. *What a coincidence. Out of all the places Les could have parked his Land Rover. Well it's the biggest marker that I've ever used, but I can't be distracted, I'm going to stick to the plotting system; it works.*

Alex walked back to the SUV, collected his equipment and went back to the plot. The afternoon session proved fruitless – modern screws, a couple of bolts, ring pulls and bottle tops. *This is so frustrating, but it's been a good day though. I wonder if our nighthawks will revisit.*

After packing up all his equipment, Alex left the field and, on his way back, called into the local village shop. He pushed open the door of the shop and a little bell tinkled. *This shop never ceases to amaze me. There are cameras everywhere, a cash point, the latest electronic checkouts with scanning, and then they have the oldest form of early warning device going, a bell fitted at the top of the doorframe that rings when the door opens to strike it.*

As Alex stepped inside, he noticed a man hobbling along on crutches, making his way to the door – it was Ian, the suspected nighthawk and self-confessed 'in it for the money' man. The two men looked at each other. Alex felt sorry for Ian, who looked in a bad state, unshaven, and with a large heavy-looking plaster cast covering most of his right leg, and he looked as if he was in pain.

'What happened to you?' asked Alex.

Ian let out a big sigh and said, 'Car crash last Thursday on the motorway; in a pile-up. Multiple breaks in the leg.'

'Sorry to hear that,' said Alex, but Ian didn't reply and began to walk towards the exit.

Alex took him by the arm. 'Look Ian, I'm sorry. It's been playing on my mind about how I spoke to you last week. It was out of character, but I just get a bit possessive, you know.'

Alex was shocked to see that Ian had a tear in his eye as he replied, 'No problem.' Ian released himself from Alex's grip and left the shop.

Alex picked up a bar of chocolate and three packets of plain crisps and went to the counter. 'That was a bad do last week that Ian was involved in,' he said to the shopkeeper, a large rotund woman with a ruddy complexion.

'It's got even worse for him today,' the shopkeeper said. 'He told me his wife has just died. He's just come from the hospital. She was in the car when they crashed. It's so sad … so, so sad. She was six months pregnant.'

Alex left the shop with a heavy heart, half hoping, half not, that he may see Ian walking down the road, but there was no trace. Instead of going straight home, Alex called in to see Reverend Jill at the rectory. He explained fully to her about the heated meeting with Ian in the field the previous week and what was said, and then about the subsequent nighthawking problems.

'I thought he was a thief, Jill, and more or less told him so.'

'Sometimes it pays to keep our thoughts to ourselves,' said Jill. 'You may still think it in your head, but even if he was guilty, should we treat him any differently when there are plenty of people out there willing to, or having to do so, because it's their job, such as the police and prison officials?'

After a short prayer for Ian and his family, Jill lightened the mood. 'Now tell me about your finds.'

Nearly an hour later, and after a coffee and slice of cake, Alex drove the ten-minute journey home from Jill's. He felt tired, not just because of the physical aspect of the day, but the emotional side of meeting Ian and finding out about his wife, the damage caused by the nighthawks and the permanent feeling of being watched. *Tuesday Club tomorrow; out with the lads.*

When he arrived home, Karen and Louise were busy in the kitchen.

'Hi Dad,' said Louise.

'Hi Lou,' he replied, before walking over to kiss Karen on the neck.

'Have you had a good day love?' she asked.

'Yes, do you want to know all about it?'

'Yes, if there are finds involved.'

'There are.'

'Then continue.'

'Give me ten minutes,' Alex said, 'I'm just going up for a shower.'

Karen could read Alex like an open book, and she could tell he was troubled. 'Do you want a glass of wine with your tea?' she asked.

'Yes please,' he replied as he left the room.

That evening Alex explained the day's events, including the nighthawk's visit, the Land Rover, Ian's shocking accident, and then he went to get his finds out of his jacket pocket. He brought them in and sat down next to Karen on the sofa. She picked up the bag containing the four musket balls and noticed a small piece of white wax paper attached.

'Is this a find as well?' she asked, holding the paper between her fingers. 'A Bonds toffee wrapper?' she added, smiling.

'Well that was in one of the holes that the nighthawk had kindly left.'

Karen screwed the sweet wrapper up and thrust it into Alex's shirt pocket. He was busy handling the stirrup and looking at it from all angles.

'That's amazing,' said Karen. 'It's in beautiful condition, and still with some leather attached.'

'I know. I think it was in an anaerobic layer. The clay is very thick, and in some parts only a few inches below the surface, so they obviously don't plough as deep. Do you remember the anaerobic layer at Vindolanda where they found a lot of the Roman writing tablets and other domestic items in an absolutely amazing condition?'

'So, you think the same conditions might apply in Claybarn Field?'

'Well obviously the finds are more modern, but they're still over three hundred and fifty years old. This Y-shaped rifle stand and the stirrup, I think when they're cleaned will be as they were left all those years ago. They were trodden into clay or somehow became covered to the point were no air could enter, so in effect preserved.'

When they had finished admiring the finds, Alex put them back into their zip-up bags. Karen changed the subject. 'So, I presume it's Tuesday Club tomorrow?'

'It is. We're ferrying across the Mersey, and as the terminal happens to be near to the museum, I can collect last week's finds and take in the coins in the pouch and today's finds.'

'You're getting a nice little collection together here,' said Karen. 'Thought about donating it to the museum to enhance our current collection?'

'No. Anything related to the Civil War I'm going to display in the church, and I've got the green light from Les the landowner and Reverend Chaplow.'

Karen rolled her eyes, as Alex continued. 'I've still got Ian on my mind; losing his pregnant wife like that, shocking business. I don't agree with nighthawking but maybe he was just trying to make some money for their new baby.'

'Maybe he was,' replied Karen, 'but it was a terrible accident, and not something you should dwell on.'

Alex, though, was lost in thought. *Wait a minute. Ian had his accident on Thursday, which means he can't be the person who was nighthawking that night or who tried Friday's scare tactics.*

The following day Alex went to Liverpool with his bothers as planned. They visited the museum first, delivered his latest finds and collected the finds that he had left for identification the previous week.

During the trip across the Mersey to the Wirral and back, the weather initially was reasonable. The sky was grey, and the air was cold but, importantly, the sea was calm. However, as they came into dock it started to rain, so as they left the ferry the three of them made a dash to a local hostelry that served good food and fine coffee.

During lunch Alex explained to his brothers about the problems that had occurred at Claybarn Field and that he thought someone was trying to warn him off. On hearing this, both Thomas and Derek decided that, because they were both free the next day, they would go with Alex and offer a hand. After initially saying that he didn't need any support, Alex gave in and agreed. *Maybe I could use this extra muscle to strike whilst the iron is hot and dig out the strange L-shaped underground construction.* He was looking forward to the three of them working together again and had promised to provide tea and sandwiches as recompense for their exertions, and for the stiffness that they would be feeling for a few days afterwards.

It was another enjoyable Tuesday Club success for the brothers Helsby. Claybarn Field, though, was never far from Alex's thoughts. That evening he was keen to prepare for the following day, so he loaded the SUV with a couple of extra spades, a mattock and a wheelbarrow. With his toolbox and a few other bits and pieces the boot was just about full.

Later that evening he was sitting watching TV when his mobile rang. It was his son Peter, who had heard from his mum about the finds and wanted to know more. When Alex informed him of the finds and the site, Peter said he would try to call in the following morning, as he had booked a day's holiday. *Wow, all this extra labour suddenly.* Alex suggested that Peter should bring wellington boots, wet weather gear and a spade, to which Peter replied, 'Oh, I'm only coming to have a look.'

After a good night's sleep, Alex was woken by Karen with a mug of coffee and a round of toast and butter. 'Thank you,' he said.

'You're welcome. Your turn tomorrow.'

Derek and Thomas arrived at Alex's house at 9.15 a.m., each bearing a spade and a pair of wellington boots. With all the equipment thrown in there was definitely no more room in the SUV. The huge bag of sandwiches and two thermos flasks of coffee, made by Karen, were rested on the back seat.

The brothers set off, and fifteen minutes later were in Claybarn Field, where the sun was shining as the clouds cleared. As they drove up the trackway towards the Land Rover, Alex's heart sank. As he looked right into the field, he could see the telltale signs of illegal digging, several small mounds of earth, not just in the decoy plot but at random, just anywhere. *So much for the Land Rover idea to keep people away.*

He continued driving up the trackway and came to a halt, more or less nose to nose with the rusty old Land Rover. They jumped out of the SUV and went to the rear hatch, where Alex passed out the wellington boots.

'I just want to have a quick look to see what damage the nighthawks have done,' Alex told his brothers. 'I'll take a few photographs to show Les later, then I'll quickly sweep over the holes and the spoil heaps, if you two don't mind doing the backfilling.'

'Okay,' came the reply.

It took about an hour for the three of them to sweep and backfill what turned out to be twenty-one holes. There were no finds, other than a couple of Bonds toffee sweet wrappers that Alex stuffed into his jacket pocket.

As they were heading back to the SUV, Derek asked, 'I presume they've dug something up from each of those holes?'

'Worst case scenario yes,' replied Alex. 'I'm feeling really annoyed about it, but other than sleeping here all night and guarding the field, there's nothing I can do, and I'm not going to do that.'

'I don't blame you,' said Thomas. 'It's up to the landowner or farmer to adequately protect the land. These fields are wide open; I mean you can see evidence of fly tipping in the field entrance just off the road, so people are coming and going as they please.'

'I know, you're right,' said Alex, 'but I'm resigned to the fact that we just have to find what we can while we can, and accept that some people do this for personal financial gain.'

'I wouldn't say no to a bit of personal financial gain,' said Derek, gesturing by rubbing his thumb and forefinger together, with a smile on his face. He had lightened the mood somewhat with his comment.

Back at the SUV Alex explained about the L-shaped structure, telling his brothers what he thought it was and where he thought it was. They all decided that it would be a good idea to reposition the SUV at ninety degrees to the Land Rover to make another L-shaped structure, but this time for privacy reasons, to keep their little excavation from the public, and prying eyes.

Alex had calculated on Google Earth a triangulation point using two trees on the boundary to the centre of the proposed dig in the L shape. He had marked the measurements on the photo grid. Now using a laser measure, he carried out the same exercise on site to prove they were standing on X marks the spot. The only difficult bit was getting a measure over the roof of the Land Rover and through the hedgerow, but eventually it was achieved with a door open and standing on a rusty door sill. According to Alex the actual measurements were within one and a half metres of the Google Earth photograph measurements, so they were in the right position and so were the vehicles.

Before they started digging, they sat down in the SUV and drank coffee. All three appeared happy.

Alex had that feeling that he hadn't had for several years, a feeling that when the three of them were together they made things happen.

Chapter 7

The Enclosure

ALEX ROUGHLY marked out an area for Derek and Thomas to dig, using his trowel as a gouge. 'If you two start the digging, when we reach clay, bring it out in squares about the width of your spade but only half a width deep. That will give the metal detector a chance to see through the clay. Anything thicker and we'll potentially be missing out on finds. I'm hoping we come across some sort of structure. It could be stone, brick, wood or anything.

'There's a possibility it could be a defensive measure from the Civil War, a post for the turnpike road, or both. Either way it looks like some sort of open enclosure with its angle facing north in parallel with Moorsdale Lane. Okay, let's start nice and slowly and see how we go.'

Derek and Thomas started at the opposite end of a trench that was designed to cut across both walls at the angle of the enclosure and cover approximately four metres. The topsoil was removed with ease and was transported by Alex via buckets to a spoil heap only five metres away. He then quickly swept over the deposits for any finds, but there was nothing in the topsoil other than ring pulls and an old piece of car number plate that had probably been deliberately thrown over the wall into the field.

When the brothers came to the clay level, the whole process slowed dramatically. The consistency of the clay proved problematic, being very dense, very firm and very heavy. Derek and Thomas stuck to the plan and extracted the clay in squares the size of a spade head, with a thickness of approximately seventy-five to a hundred millimetres, which roughly equated to two house bricks side by side.

Alex decided to try to break each square brick down to bite-sized pieces using his trowel, before quickly sweeping over the pieces for any finds. This was also hard work and slow going, and he quickly gave up on the trowel in favour of a spade.

Before long, lunchtime had arrived, and the brothers returned to the SUV. Alex took the opportunity to message Les with a photograph of more holes, courtesy of the nighthawks, and the prize finds of Bonds toffee wrappers. Over lunch the brothers were quite subdued; the work was harder than they expected, and they were all finding it tough.

'You two carry on with your lunch, I'm just going to put a few bores down into the clay to see if I can find anything solid,' said Alex.

'Don't you think it's solid enough?' replied Thomas, with a laugh. Derek joined in.

Alex took a small hammer and a 600mm-long metal drill bit from his toolbox. With a 12mm diameter he had found it quite handy in the past when searching for any underground constructions or obstructions. Standing over the shallow trench his attention was absorbed by what looked like a change of colour in the clay. *It looks like a discolouration of the clay at two separate points across the trench. That slightly darker stuff could be significant.*

He bent down and slowly tapped the drill bit into the first of the darker sections within the clay. At a depth of approximately five centimetres, the drill bit hit something firm but not metallic. He then tapped the drill bit into the second darker section, which was less than two metres away. Again, at a depth of approximately five centimetres he felt the drill bit hit something with a quiet thud. He then carried out a couple of sample bores at random in the lighter clay within the trench, and the drill bit just went further and further into the ground. There was then the problem of extracting it from the clay, so his toolbox came in handy again. With the use of an adjustable wrench, he was able to extract the drill bit. *Those dark areas must be timber walls or supports, possibly for the enclosure. If they're seventeenth century original, there could be lots of finds inside there … and immediately around the outside if it was a defensive position.*

Alex went back to talk to his brothers, and they discussed how to continue, agreeing that to reveal the top of the enclosure in its entirety would be a good idea. Then, as phase two, they would excavate the area within for any finds.

The brothers set to work after lunch, and it didn't take them long to reveal a timber structure as predicted. The timbers were at ninety degrees to each other, and the projection point was parallel with the road and, in effect, pointing towards Moors Field. Each length of timber was approximately two metres in length; early indicators showed that they consisted of rows of horizontal timbers stacked on top of each other, kept in place by two vertical stakes on each side, but until they excavated a little deeper, they wouldn't be able to confirm this either way.

Alex asked his brothers to excavate one side of the wall each at the same time so there was no bias and unnecessary burden of earth weight to one side of the wall. Meanwhile, he started another small spoil pile to distinguish which find, if any, came out from which area.

It didn't take long before Derek, digging outside of the enclosure, spotted a musket ball embedded in the clay, its grey metallic colour standing out clearly against the terracotta brown and orange background. Derek was delighted; it was, after all, his first ever find. Alex did the usual, bagging the item up and recording its grid reference number on the photo plan and bag. The brothers then went for an afternoon break and finished off the last of the coffee from the thermos flask.

'Are we alright digging here? This is going to end up quite a hole if you want to see this enclosure you're looking for,' said Thomas.

'I know,' replied Alex. 'I'll send another message to Les, just to make sure he's okay with us doing this.

I think we'll be okay because we're over in the corner and just on the edge of the sowing area.' He then sent a text message to Les.

The brothers went back to work. The weather had changed a little now. Gone was the mid-afternoon sunshine of a beautiful spring day. The temperature had dropped, and the skies were grey. 'I think the fog may be on its way back, so let's crack on,' said Alex.

'Aye aye, cap'n,' replied Derek. More musket balls were found and bagged, and even Thomas had his first musket ball find as part of a group of three, which looked unfired. It was noticeable that all the musket ball finds on the outside of the enclosure were damaged in some way, as if they had struck something, but there was also the possibility of plough damage.

Thomas drew Alex's attention. 'Alex, look at this.' Alex bent over to get a better view of what exactly Thomas was pointing at, pulling the trowel from his jacket pocket and gently scraping the clay away. He recognised it through its shape.

'Oh, what a beauty,' said Alex excitedly. 'It's got to be a powder flask. This would have contained a soldier's gunpowder for his musket, and it's in amazing condition.' He lifted the item from the clay and held it out for his brothers to see. They simultaneously touched the item, admiring it.

'It's actually made from a cow horn. There's probably an engraving on it,' said Alex.

Derek rubbed the side of the horn after spitting on his fingers. 'You're right,' he said. 'It looks like a man standing beneath a tree ready to fire his musket. Very appropriate. It's actually a beautiful piece of work.'

Alex took hold of the item. 'This looks like a silver tip on the sharp end, and the fitting on the other end will contain an internal thread. This screw plug in the top means it could still have its contents. I don't know anything about explosives, but this needs to be handled with care. It could be unstable.' The brothers were silent.

'We can't take it away with us then. It's too dangerous,' said Thomas.

'Okay, let's bag it, mark it and then re-bury it in a location that we can come back to,' suggested Alex.

It was the first time that day that he felt vulnerable again. He started to scan the hedgerows, which were getting thicker and greener by the day. He was suddenly conscious of the possibility of being watched.

Alex warned his brothers. 'We need to be aware that we could be being watched. We must use the cover of the vehicles to hide as much of our activities as possible. As we're standing here, we can't be seen at the field entrance, so bearing this in mind, the hole needs to be behind us, away from the ploughing area, but making sure that we still use the cover of the vehicles.'

'I can see just the spot,' said Thomas. Alex placed the powder flask in a large zip-up bag and entered the relevant details on the outside of the bag and on his photo grid.

Thomas cut a large enough hole out of the wild grass just in front of a large squat hawthorn bush. He took the bagged item from Alex, placed it in the hole, covered it with a small amount of backfill, then placed the square of wild grass turf in the top of the hole.

Alex placed a small stone at the location and took a grid reference reading. 'Let's get back to the enclosure,' he said. *We don't want to draw any attention to that spot. Mind you, this fog is affording some cover and it's getting thicker.*

Back at the enclosure, Derek found several musket balls very quickly. 'Who needs a metal detector?' he shouted. 'A good pair of eyes is all you need.'

On the inside of the enclosure Thomas had excavated to a depth of approximately thirty centimetres, and the hole had a nice defined shape, with the timber wall forming one of the four sides, the other three with a smooth clay finish.

Alex thought he saw a small amount of discolouration on one of the clay walls. 'Thomas, can I just get in there for a second to run my metal detector around,' he said.

'You don't need that. Just use your eyes,' Thomas replied jokingly.

'I have. That's why I'm now using my metal detector,' Alex said, with a smug look on his face. He stepped into the hole with his detector, which immediately signalled a ferrous metal hit between his feet. Because he was wearing the headphones around his neck, the others became immediately aware of the find, as they could hear it through the speakers.

'What's that?' asked Thomas.

'Something iron-based, but a very strong and large signal,' said Alex. *This looks interesting.* 'Can you just pass me that trowel,' he said, pointing at it. Thomas passed it to him, and Alex pushed the point in. It stopped after a very short distance. He began to scrape away the layers in one area to reveal what looked like a flat piece of metal. The more he scraped away the larger it got.

Thomas passed him a spade, and Alex quickly revealed what looked like a large sheet of metal plate, approximately seventy-five centimetres square. He tapped it with the spade. *Rock solid. This is really mysterious. I wonder whether it has sides to it.* He pushed his hands to the edge of the plate, and carefully bent his fingers around the corners.

'It looks like it's got sides.' Alex confirmed this when he was eventually able to run his fingers all the way around, after some more spade work. 'It's a solid construction. Could be some sort of a container.'

'What about some sort of farming equipment or an animal trough,' suggested Derek.

'I'm not so sure,' replied Alex. 'This looks and feels like it may be very heavy. It could even be cast iron.'

'Cast iron makes me think of heavy industry,' said Thomas. 'And there used to be a lot of it only a few miles away; locomotives, ammunitions, tanks for the war, that sort of thing. But out here in the sticks, it seems so out of place. Shall we just ignore it and go around it? After all, the original idea was to reveal the construction we now call the enclosure.'

'You're right,' agreed Alex. 'But if you two don't mind digging out a little more so I can at least make an educated guess at what it actually is …'

Thomas looked at Derek, and Derek looked at Thomas; they both jokingly shook their heads, then Derek said, 'Just this once.'

'Thank you,' said Alex, then just for a second the three of them stood there with their arms around each other's shoulders, just like the good old days.

Alex wanted to clear as much clay as he could from around the metal object, and he never intended to leave it in the ground. The three of them worked on adjacent sides until Thomas shouted, 'Stop. Look at this.' The three men were bending down, looking at the side that Thomas had been clearing.

'It looks like a safe,' said Thomas.

Alex looked at it in amazement. 'I'd say so too.' *I can't believe it. I've never felt so excited in all of my life. I hope there's something inside.* He felt his heart racing as he leaned forward to touch the front of the safe. It was in very good condition and was pockmarked with rivet heads, with a fine engraved series of letters on the front. There was also a brass handle and escutcheon plate covering a keyhole.

'This is amazing,' said Derek. 'Presuming it's locked, it could be an absolute pig to unlock.'

'Where do you think it's come from?' asked Thomas. 'And how old do you think it is?'

'I haven't got a clue,' said Alex. 'Let's just try to get it out if we can.'

The levels of excitement between the three men grew considerably, but they remained quiet and dug deep on every side of the safe until it was fully exposed and was sitting on its side on an island made of clay.

It was a complete cube in shape, with a black hammered metal finish that covered the entire safe.

It was then trimmed off with the brass handle and escutcheon plate. Alex tried the handle, not expecting the door to swing open, which it didn't.

'Okay,' said Alex, 'let's see if we can lift it out of this hole.' They each got a grip of the safe on their own sides by sliding their fingers into the clay beneath it, leaving their thumbs on the outside. It took a mammoth effort to just lift the safe over the lip of the hole, before placing it down on the surface mud.

'Well we can't leave it here,' said Derek. 'Somehow we have to get it in the back of your SUV Alex; we have to find a way to get it in and out safely.'

'What a find,' said Thomas excitedly. 'We must get this back to yours Alex, and get it opened.'

'I know,' Alex replied. 'We just have to figure out a way of doing it. I'm just going to call Karen.' Alex dialled Karen's mobile.

'Hi, it's me. You're not going to believe this, but we've found a safe in the middle of the field. It's locked but, somehow, we have to try to get it back to ours to see if we can open it. I'm going to need the two wooden scaffolding planks out of the garage, and I think the rope might come in handy.'

'Whoa, slow down,' said Karen. 'I'm not bringing your stuff up to you.'

'Why not?' said Alex, getting annoyed.

'Because our son is here, so I'll send him up.'

'Tell him to bring the two planks, the rope and a pair of wellies.'

'Okay, I will. It's very exciting,' said Karen.

'I know, and it looks very old.'

'Do you think it could be Civil War plunder that literally fell off the back of a horse and cart?' asked Karen.

'I don't know, but I'm going to find out,' said Alex, and rang off.

Twenty minutes later, Peter arrived at the entrance to Claybarn Field, having followed his mother's directions. The fog was dense as he slowly and methodically made his way up the hill, but when

179

the wheels of his Audi began to spin, he decided to stop there and walk the rest of the way. He slipped the two half-lengths of scaffolding planks back through the open passenger window and out through the open rear hatch.

The three brothers had heard a car entering the field and were walking down the trackway when they saw the Audi. Peter was just pulling on his wellington boots when they approached. After the initial pleasantries and the shaking of hands, they began to walk up the hill, Peter carrying a coil of rope, and Thomas and Derek a timber plank each.

'Sorry, I got stuck in the mud on the incline, otherwise I'd have been closer,' said Peter apologetically.

'It's okay,' replied Alex. 'It's just up here.' The shape of the Land Rover, then the SUV, slowly appeared through the fog.

'Mum was telling me about all of your finds, and today the safe. It's fantastic, so exciting,' said Peter.

'I know,' said Alex, 'but the main thing now is that we get that safe back home. We're lucky today that this fog has shrouded our work, otherwise people would be wanting to know what's going on, and we have a problem with nighthawks.'

'I heard about that. Mum told me. Any ideas who's doing it?' Peter asked.

'I thought I did, but I was wrong, so in answer to your question, I haven't got a clue.'

The four men stood around the safe. The SUV had been repositioned with the rear hatch open and the two planks positioned on the incline from its rear to just in front of where the safe lay.

'Right, we need to manoeuvre the safe on to the two planks,' said Alex. 'When it's fully on the planks, and we're taking its weight, Peter, can you get in the back of the SUV and try your best to stop the planks from sliding up, because as we push the safe, they'll probably want to move too.'

'Yes, okay Dad.'

The four men did exactly as planned, and with a great amount of effort they managed to push the safe up the planks and into the back of the SUV, which by now had lowered considerably due to the weight of pressure on its suspension, and also sinkage into the mud and clay beneath it. The men cheered and punched the air in delight, all exclaiming, 'Yes! Yes!'

Before the hole was backfilled, Alex did another sweep where the safe had been lying and, to his astonishment, he found three more metal-tipped and, more importantly, sealed cow horn black powder flasks. These items joined the other buried flask in the marked location.

The excavation holes were backfilled, grid reference numbers recorded and finds recorded on the photo grid. The vehicles were loaded up and ready to leave. Thomas decided to go with Peter to reduce the load in the SUV.

'See you back at ours,' shouted Alex to Peter and Thomas.

'Okay, but I might need you in a minute to push me out of the mud,' replied Peter.

Alex fired up the SUV. Derek was in the passenger seat rubbing his hands together. 'I was just thinking,' he said. 'This feels a bit like stealing, and it's the first time in my life ...'

'It's okay,' assured Alex, interrupting him. 'This is all in agreement with the landowner, Les Pritchard.'

'But what if it was stolen in a burglary and dumped in the field?'

'Well, if we find evidence of who it belonged to, we'll give it back, but honestly Derek, it looks very old. I think it's been in the ground for hundreds of years. Look, if it makes you feel better, when we get home, I'll call Les and let him know exactly what we've found.'

'Yes, I would feel better Alex.'

'I was going to call him anyway,' said Alex.

Initially, the SUV struggled to move, but once it made its way out of the hollows created by its own tyres it moved slowly down the trackway.

The fog was dense; it wasn't swirling around, it just sat like a heavy cloud of cold vapour, and in the SUV headlights it looked like fine drizzle, and rendered the lights useless as the light just reflected back.

As expected, they soon came across Peter's Audi. They both jumped out of the SUV, noticing that Thomas was caked in mud. 'The back wheels just keep spinning. They can't get any purchase in the mud,' Thomas said.

The three brothers managed to push the car out of the quagmire, as Peter steered it in reverse towards the entrance. Both vehicles made it out of the field, but Alex's SUV complained all the way back to his house, with unusual creaks and vibrations.

When they arrived, he reversed up the drive and opened the hatch. Peter pulled up on the drive next to him. Alex pressed the switch on his garage's electric shutter fob, and it rolled itself up before clicking to a stop. Karen opened the front door, then stepped out to see what the four of them were standing there looking at. 'Thank god you weren't stopped by the police,' she joked.

Chapter 8

The Grand Opening

THE FOUR men managed to slide the safe on its back down the planks using a rope that was wrapped around it and fed back through two hooped anchor points in the rear of the SUV. This method gave them a degree of control on its descent, but it still hit the garage floor with a thump.

'Has anyone heard or felt anything moving inside the safe at all?' asked Alex. Everyone just shook their heads. *It's looking as if it may be empty after all.* He filled a bucket of water from the tap in the corner of the garage and grabbed a sponge that was wedged between the tap handle and the wall. He wiped the safe down after damping the sponge. The so-called pattern on the front door of the safe was, in fact, a series of ornate letters inscribed and overlapping.

'What do you think it is Alex?' Derek asked. 'The Bank of England?'

'I can certainly see an S and a K, possibly an N and O, and another O and what could be a T. So, it could be the bank of SKNOOT, that well-known high street financial establishment,' said Alex, which made the others snigger. 'How are we going to get into it? Anyone any ideas?' he asked.

Derek stepped forward and looked at the keyhole closely. 'Well I don't think we'll be able to pick the lock for a number of reasons. There's the sheer size of the mechanism; this is a big one. It's probably degraded and, looking at the size of it, it looks like a bank grade or jeweller's safe. If you look carefully down the opening side of the door, you'll see a small gap about the same width as at the hinge side to allow the door to swing open. And if you look through the gap and in line with the keyhole you can just see a small section of the bolt, which is thrown into the locked position into the keep in the frame of the safe. The hinges are internal, so there's nothing to work on. Even looking in the recess of the full length of the door there's nothing. I think our only option is to cut through the bolt.'

'How will you do it?' asked Alex.

Derek said, 'I've got an angle grinder at home that allows the cutting blade to be rotated slightly off the perpendicular, which allows cutting to take place in narrow spaces and at acute angles from a workable position.'

'How long do you think it will take to cut through?' Alex asked.

'That's a difficult one Alex, and it depends upon on the type of metal the bolt is made from, and to what extent it's been hardened. We also have to take into consideration the fact that when using the angle grinder in confined spaces, it's impossible to apply the same degree of force or weight to the cutting edge, so it could take me five minutes or five hours, but I'll get through it.'

'What about the contents?' asked Peter.

'Well, if there's anything in there such as documents, there's always the possibility that a stray spark could find its way in. It's pretty difficult to tell how tight fitting the door is going to be, but what I could do is pack the gap with modelling clay or putty, or something similar. I'll just leave the area around the bolt free for the cutter, so that should reduce the odds of a potential fire inside.'

'Derek, it sounds like a plan to me. When can you do it?' asked Alex.

'I'll come back first thing in the morning. I should have all the gear at home.'

'That's brilliant, thank you,' said Alex. 'Is everyone up for tea and something to eat?'

'Yes' came the unanimous reply, so the four them had tea and a large plate of ham sandwiches, followed by cake, biscuits and more tea. Karen was the grateful hostess, as she knew that without their help, Alex would probably have not even found the safe, never mind got it home.

They were excited about the find and had all come to the same conclusion that the black powder was strategically positioned in an attempt to blow the safe open. So, whoever had stolen the safe had packed the explosives underneath with a small amount on top but never had the opportunity or the time to complete the job. Was that because they were enveloped in the heat of a battle, maybe the English Civil War? So were the safe contents the spoils of war, or was it just an empty safe?

Derek and Thomas left Alex's home, promising to be back the next morning. Unfortunately for Peter, he had to go to work, but had asked for photographs and updates the minute the safe was opened, unless it was empty.

After everyone had left, Alex and Karen went into the garage, and even Louise extracted herself from her bedroom to look at the star find. Karen had queried their right to extract the safe in the first place, and was very unsure about the plans to open it. However, she did admit to wanting to see what was inside.

Alex decided to call Les. *It's technically his, as we found it on his land.* Les was his usual self; once he knew all about the safe, where it was in the field, how big it was, what condition it was in, what colour it was, how deep it was and what condition his field was in, he said, 'Just get the thing opened,' in his no-nonsense manner.

That evening Alex was tired but excited. He couldn't wait for the morning to come. He methodically wrote down what to do as the safe was opened, one of the items on his list being to ensure uninterrupted footage was taken as soon as it was opened until, or if, any items were found. He would have to allocate this task to Thomas, as Derek would be working on the safe. Everything would then need to be bagged, listed and photographed.

He was so tired that he fell asleep, then awoke at 3 a.m. still in his lounge chair. He stood and made his way to the stairs. *My back is so sore. I shouldn't have fallen asleep in my chair.* He made his way up to bed, sneaked in beside Karen, and fell straight back to sleep.

Chapter 9

19 August 1648

A S THE battle of Winwick Pass, otherwise known as Red Bank, raged, Oliver Cromwell and a company of horse had outflanked the Scots Royalists and continued to Warrington town in pursuit of the Scots rearguard horse that had fled. Cromwell had given Captain Clarkson, along with a foot battalion, strict instructions to follow him, not to engage the enemy, then to hold at Winwick's church to form a rearguard trap on the rest of the predicted fleeing Royalists.

A post rider had left Oliver Cromwell's quarters at Church Street in Warrington that afternoon. In his possession was a note written in longhand on a small roll of rustic paper by Cromwell himself. His destination was St Oswald's Church at Winwick, and the recipient was Captain Clarkson.

The letter instructed Clarkson that the contents of the church safe were to be secured to prevent damage or looting and returned to him in person at his quarters in Church Street. It mentioned that the Rector, Charles Herle, was in Scotland as part of a team working on behalf of the Parliamentarians to negotiate a conclusion to the war with the Royalist enemy, and that the whereabouts of the safe key was unknown. It instructed Clarkson to open the safe by fair means or foul.

The post rider had battled the elements of torrential rain and had difficulty in avoiding some of the renegades who were wandering the streets, looting and running from Parliamentarian law enforcers on horse and foot. However, he had covered the distance in twenty minutes and handed the note to Clarkson in person.

Clarkson sat in the corner of the vestry reading the letter from Cromwell. The safe was free-standing in the opposite corner. In fact, it was probably one of the few dry spots in the church, and this was more by luck than judgement.

The church generally was in a poor state of repair. Most of the windows were missing, as the lead had been stripped out to make musket balls. The roof wasn't much better; rain poured in through the nave roof and was running down the bell tower steps, flooding the area.

Several soldiers had made it to the bell tower roof, keeping lookout from an elevated vantage point; other foot soldiers were acting as sentries in the churchyard just inside the stone perimeter wall.

A large packhorse and cart were manoeuvring in the sodden churchyard, coming to a halt at the double west doors of the tower. The doors were flung open, the flood waters poured out and a huge barrel-chested man with a rope strewn around his shoulders attached to a large safe that was being pushed by a group of men under Clarkson's orders, lifted the safe on to the back of the cart. The horse showed its displeasure with a large nasal snort and the slight shifting of its hooves.

The group of men walked alongside the horse as it attempted to exit the churchyard. They were looking for the gravel path. The cart's wheels dug deep into the grass as it turned, and the horse had great difficulty gaining any forward motion. It veered slightly to the left, further away from the path that was its goal.

The soldiers took matters into their own hands and started to kick down gravestones in an attempt to make an exit via the shortest possible route. If anything, it made it harder for the horse to pull the cart, as its wheels kept dropping off the edge of one of the lying headstones then had to rise over another.

It was a very slow process, and at one point it appeared that one of the wheels was coming away from the frame of the cart until the barrel-chested man appeared with a large lump of stone and struck the wheel and forced it to return it to its correct position on its axle.

When the horse and cart had made it to the path, it made short work of crossing Moorsdale Lane and headed up the bank into Claybarn Field. Very quickly the cart came to a standstill, as its heavy wheels sunk through the mud and soil into the firm clay beneath it. One of the men struck the horse with a tree branch picked up from the road. The horse heaved with all its heart, its shoulders and neck bulging with muscle and vein. The animal was blowing heavily now, and it was obvious that it could go no further.

The barrel-chested man ordered the men to lift the safe to the nearby turnpike post. Once in position, one of the men dug out an area in the clay beneath the safe door and inserted the black powder flasks. They had just positioned one on top of the safe when voices could be heard coming from the north in Moorsdale Lane. Men were shouting 'sanctuary, sanctuary, head for the church'. It was the Royalists on the run from Red Bank and heading straight for them.

Clarkson's men tried as best they could to hide the safe by covering it with mud and clay, but they had left their muskets in the church, so they turned and ran. Some of the Royalists on retreat had stopped and rearmed, and Clarkson's men were sitting ducks, as their bodies were hit with hard heavy lead musket balls. They never even made it across Moorsdale Lane; they were all killed.

The sentries in the churchyard and on the church tower began to open fire on the Royalists, who fled into the trees near the turnpike post. Huge explosions could then be heard from the direction of Red Bank and, a second later, further noise nearby as Parliamentarian cannonballs landed on and amongst the fleeing men. The volley continued smashing branches off trees. Cannonballs that landed in the field sent a huge amount of dirt into the air, covering the men. Some trees, the road, even the turnpike post had disappeared under the detritus of war.

Some Royalists reappeared with their hands up as the rest of Clarkson's battalion rounded them up, marched them to the church and imprisoned them under guard.

That afternoon there was a steady stream of Royalists who were imprisoned in the church. Cromwell's plan was a success, if slightly tarnished by the fact that the church safe was lost somewhere in a field and the only men who knew where it was had been killed. Clarkson had asked his sentries in the churchyard and even the soldiers in the tower, who must have seen where it had been buried, but under the green canopy of the trees nothing could be seen.

Clarkson sent a foot soldier over to Claybarn Field to do a reconnoitre of the area, but the young man returned looking rather the worse for wear, having seen several bodies, including the horse, which looked as if it had been the victim of a direct hit by a cannonball. As for the cart, it had disintegrated, and there was no sign of the safe.

Chapter 10

The Safe Contents

A LEX WAS rudely awoken the next day at 7.45 a.m. as Karen threw open the bedroom curtains and the sunlight burst through the venetian blinds straight on to his face. He screwed up his eyes then placed a forearm across his face.

'Oh, the beauty of a south-facing rear garden,' said Karen. 'Sunshine all day long.'

'Okay, okay,' said Alex.

This was a long-standing joke between them, as Alex had forgone many other houses favoured by Karen for the sake of this house and its south-facing rear garden, and Karen had never let him forget it.

Later that morning, Alex was in the garage when Derek and Thomas arrived at more or less the same time. Derek had reversed his car right up to the garage and was unloading a small metal toolbox, followed by what Alex assumed was his angle grinder. He saw Alex looking at the grinder. 'Super-thin abrasive disk, lots of sparks, but the quickest cut,' he said.

'Yes, nice piece of kit,' said Alex. 'And good morning to you both.'

'Good morning,' the brothers replied.

'I can't wait to see if there's anything in this safe,' added Thomas.

'Me neither,' replied Alex, 'but if you don't mind, I have an important job for you Thomas. We need for evidence purposes to film everything once the safe is open. We don't want anybody being accused of misappropriation. Everything that comes out of that safe has got to be recorded. It's a self-preservation issue. Let's keep it transparent, just in case.'

'Yes, I understand that,' agreed Thomas.

Derek continued to prepare himself for the cutting of the safe. His protective eyewear and gloves were in place. He plugged in the angle grinder and presented the disk to the gap between the safe outer case and its door. 'That's promising,' he said. 'This thin disk fits in the gap nicely, so I won't need to make any adjustments. I'm ready to go.'

Alex gave the thumbs up and Thomas held up Alex's mobile, indicating he was ready to record. Derek pulled the trigger and fired up the machine, which was loud, but as the disk first struck metal the noise was absolutely deafening. Then the hot shower of sparks flew up and hit the garage wall, covering the men.

Derek stopped the machine immediately. 'I think it may be a good idea if I use this.' He put the machine down, and out of his toolbox he produced a large tub of yellow play putty. 'Sorry Alex, I forgot about this.'

'You and me both,' replied Alex.

Derek started to stuff the gap around the safe door and just left the area around the lock bolt, which was sitting secure in its keep. When he had finished, he grabbed an old woollen hat from his tool bag and covered his head as much as he could without obscuring his vision. 'I think you and Thomas should wait outside; it would be safer.'

The two men retreated to the driveway and closed the garage door. Derek started immediately, and the noise from outside was loud, but no louder than the average tradesman carrying out an extension, who starts drilling at 8.30 a.m. on a Sunday morning.

Suddenly, the machine stopped, and Derek opened the garage door. A cloud of black smoke emerged, hitting the two men in their faces.

'Is it done?' asked Alex, coughing.

'No chance,' said Derek. 'I'll never get through that.'

Just for a second, Alex's heart sank with disappointment, then Derek shouted, 'Done it … piece of cake!'

All three men were smiling with joy and anticipation. 'Right, don't touch anything, I'm just going to get Karen,' said Alex.

When Alex and Karen returned, Alex said to Thomas, 'Okay, can you start recording now?'

'Okay,' said Thomas, as Alex went to grab the handle to pull the door open.

Derek stopped him, handing him a glove. 'It'll be hot.'

Alex slipped the glove on and grabbed the handle. The safe door started to open and there was a sharp metallic squeak from one of the hinges. Derek could see the door was heavy, so with his remaining gloved hand helped it to the open position until it stopped on its hinges.

'Well at least it's not empty,' said Alex, as he took hold of a dirty white canvas bag with a drawstring and a dark stain around its outside, as if it had been sitting in water. The smell was musty as expected, but the cloth appeared in reasonable condition. *There's something heavy and metallic inside*, Alex thought, then put both of his hands inside the safe and wrapped them around the bag.

'Derek, there's a piece of plywood on my wooden bench. Can you get it and hold it next to the safe so that I can transfer the bag on to the board, then the board on to the bench. I think this bag may rip.'

Thomas was recording everything as Alex put the bag on to the board, then Derek moved the board to the bench. Thomas moved in as Alex cut the bag open with a pair of scissors. They were all staggered with what they saw, and there was an audible gasp from Karen. *This is way beyond my hopes and expectations*, thought Alex.

Lying there in an open canvas shroud were several of what looked like silver items. Alex picked them out one by one and placed them on the open work bench. There were four antique Baroque-style silver chalices, with what looked like a red gemstone of considerable size in the base of each one. There were two silver ciboria-covered cups, the lids finished by a standing cross. These items again looked in the Baroque style and matched the set of chalices in design.

Next to come out was a small silver wafer box, complete with hinged lid and a beautiful design, which covered its entirety. Alex then caressed an amazing silver flagon, approximately thirty centimetres in height, its beautiful floral and leaf design covering every aspect of its exterior. It had a very ornate spout and handle.

The next and last item in the bag was contained within what looked like a choirboy's surplice, with a roughly hemmed neck and large flared sleeves. This was by far the heaviest and largest item. Alex pulled it out, still unravelling it from the surplice, then it appeared – a large gold cross on a gold stand, approximately forty-five centimetres in height. The light radiated from its pristine surface, unlike the previous items, which were all tarnished. This came out as if it had been cleaned yesterday. There was some very fine leaf work on its front. It was magnificent. *I've never seen anything as beautiful as this, never mind held it*, Alex thought.

Derek spoke quietly and with reverence. 'That's one amazing, spectacular thing.'

Karen interrupted him. 'Please, please let me hold it.' Alex passed the cross to her, warning her about its weight. She took hold of it with both hands. 'I'm totally lost for words. I know it's unusual for me, but I'm just …'

Karen never completed her sentence. The next thing she said was 'St Oswald's'. She had just turned the cross around and was looking at an ornate inscription that ran down the rear of the main column.

Thomas, now looking over her shoulder, pointed at the inscription. 'She's right … St Oswald's.'

'Do you want to hold it?' Karen asked Thomas, who was still filming.

Thomas just reached over and touched it. 'No thanks, I'm too frightened of dropping it.'

Derek, with outstretched arms, said, 'Yes please,' and took it from her hands. 'Wow, the weight of this thing. Is it solid gold?'

'I think so,' said Alex, 'seeing as gold doesn't corrode or tarnish to any great degree.'

'There will be a hallmark on it somewhere,' said Karen. 'Hallmarking originated in the 1300s, I think. Well in this country it did anyway.'

Derek took a cursory glance around the cross, then handed it back to Alex, who placed it on its back on the bench, revealing the solid gold base. 'There's some kind of mark on here,' Alex said. 'I can certainly see a crown at the very minimum.'

'That's the mark for gold,' said Karen.

Alex lifted the cross and placed it upright on the bench. He removed the remnants of the bag, so that all of the treasures were sitting there. For a few seconds they stared, as Thomas went close up with Alex's mobile phone, still recording his video.

'We've not finished yet,' Alex said, returning to the open safe.' Everyone gathered around as Alex put his hand to the bottom of the safe and pulled out what looked like several documents placed inside a fold of paper, about the size of an A4 sheet. He handled them with care, as he had all the other items. He didn't open out the plain fold of paper, he just slid the documents out from the inside, then checked the folded paper inside and out on both sides.

'I think that's just a protective sheet to keep the documents together. Its blank,' Alex said, putting it to one side on the work bench. He then selected the first few documents in the pile, which were headed 'St Oswald's Baptisms 1610–1625', and had a series of columns running down the pages, giving dates, names of the child and names of the parents. The end column looked as if it was the incumbent clergyman or their representative's name.

There was also a series of burial records dating back to 1599, and finally a quantity of what looked like marriage documents. The latter appeared to have been badly damaged by water prior to being lodged in the safe. All the documents were headed 'St Oswald's'.

'They're fantastic,' enthused Karen. 'These are documents that no one has seen, recorded or talked about in the modern era. It's like a history of the parishioners. They're unique.'

'Spoken like a good museum archivist,' said Derek.

'Can I stop recording now?' asked Thomas.

'Yes. Thanks for doing that,' replied Alex, 'and Derek, thanks for getting the safe opened. I couldn't have done any of this without your help.'

'I know,' Derek replied, 'and I have the spark burns to prove it.' They all laughed.

'Seriously though; this has got to be one of the best finds in the north of England for years,' suggested Thomas.

'Well, it doesn't match any of the famous hoard finds, such as the Staffordshire hoard, for example, but it is significant,' said Karen.

'And what do you think a find like this could be worth?' Thomas asked.

Karen considered for a moment. 'With regard to the metal items, that all depends on the valuers. Their conclusion is based on a number of things, such as the quality and grade of the metal, the value of the metals on today's market, how well it was made, how rare it is and a whole host of other criteria to formulate a final figure. But it could be worth a few hundred thousand pounds; I really don't know. With regard to the church documents, they're obviously very valuable to the church and anyone who is carrying out research.'

'I guess this all goes back to St Oswald's,' said Derek.

'Well, if their name is on it, I'd say yes,' said Karen. 'It belongs to the church.'

Derek then proceeded to look at every item in detail – the bases, the lids, the insides – then said, 'Guess what; the whole lot is marked. It's all theirs.'

'This could only happen to us,' said Thomas. 'We find a cache of gold and silver, only to find it's got the owner's name written all over it.'

'It wouldn't matter if it was all melted down,' said Derek.

'Erm, I don't think so,' Alex interjected sharply, as his brothers sniggered.

Soon after, Derek and Thomas left, promising to call Alex the next day. Alex and Karen were still standing in the garage, mesmerised, particularly by the golden cross.

'Where do we go from here?' asked Karen.

'Well, we stick to the normal procedure and report it to the finds liaison officer. It's also important that I tell them about the black powder flasks that are buried in the field, which need to be recovered safely. I'll also give Jill a call and give her the good news. I'm sure she will be around here in a flash. Then I think I'll call Les to let him know what we found in his field. Oh, and then I'll call Peter, as I promised to keep him in the loop.'

'Call him first,' suggested Karen. 'He said he wanted to know right away.'

'Yes, okay, I'll do that,' Alex agreed.

When Alex called him, Peter was absolutely delighted and said he was coming over the following evening to have a look. Even when Alex told him that he thought there was a possibility that the finds liaison team may want to collect the items before then, Peter said he was still coming.

Alex then called Les, who was, in his own words, 'chuffed', and said he would call in the next day.

Next on the list was Reverend Jill. 'Good evening Jill, it's Alex here.'

'Hi Alex.'

'Jill, you're not going to believe this, but we've made a significant find in Claybarn Field.'

'Really?' Jill replied excitedly. 'How significant?'

'Well, how about silver chalices and a gold cross for starters?'

'Oh my gosh. Praise the Lord. Is it ours?'

'I believe it is Jill. Every item is inscribed with St Oswald's.'

'I don't believe it. That's fantastic news. The missing treasures are being returned. It's just a rumour, but Oliver Cromwell was blamed for looting Church wealth in the form of treasures. He was implicated on a TV documentary several years ago, but proving or disproving the theory is impossible.'

'Well, it wasn't actually stolen so to speak,' said Alex. 'It was buried in the field in a locked safe, which was packed with explosives around the outside, but never activated.'

'How extraordinary. Can I come round to see the items in the morning?' Jill asked.

'Of course. I'll be here all day.'

Alex then decided to take some good photographs of the finds to email ahead of his telephone call to report the finds to the authorities. Using his Nikon SLR, he was able to get a good selection of quality close-up photographs. He forwarded them with his contact details to the find's liaison officer at the Museum of Liverpool. *I'll give them a call in the morning.*

That evening, Alex and Karen carried the precious items into the house and arranged them on the dining room table. Alex closed the blinds. *Better make sure the alarm is on tonight.* Later, they retired to bed early, as a sense of achievement and the contents of a bottle of French Pinot Noir washed over them.

Chapter 11

The Sanctuary Cipher

THE TELEPHONE was ringing by the bedside. Alex could hear Karen in the kitchen making breakfast, so he leaned across and picked up the handset. 'Hello,' he said.

'Alex, its Les. I'm sorry it's a bit early, but us farmers tend to rise a little earlier than most.'

'It's alright. What time are you coming round?' asked Alex.

'About fifteen minutes if that's alright with you.'

'That's fine. There'll be a cup of tea waiting for you.'

'Thanks Alex. See you shortly.' Les ended the call.

Twenty minutes later, Alex was suitably refreshed after his morning shower and was in the dining room with a mug of tea, surveying the previous day's treasure finds. Karen had just left for work when Les arrived. He was given a mug of tea, then Alex showed him through to the dining room.

'I think you'll be impressed,' said Alex. There in all its splendour on the dining table was the collection. 'I'm calling it the Claybarn find.'

'You can call it whatever you like,' said Les. 'It's magnificent.' He was drawn to the gold cross first, then he handled the chalices and the ciboria. 'I presume these are silver and the cross is gold?'

'The hallmark on each item indicates all the silverware is solid silver and the cross is solid gold,' explained Alex. 'Follow me into the garage.' They walked outside, and Alex lifted the garage door. Lying on the floor in the middle of the garage was the safe on its back with the door swung open.

'This is the beast we found in your field Les. We had to grind through the lock bolt to get it open.'

'This is a real safe cracking operation you have going on here,' Les replied with a smile. 'Does this mean I'm a rich man?' he asked, as he looked at Alex with a straight face.

I hope he doesn't think this is our treasure, Alex thought. 'You're rich anyway Les, and I was just going to say that unfortunately it's all inscribed with the name St Oswald.'

Les interrupted, 'It's okay. I know it all belongs to the church, and it should go back to where it belongs. They could sell some of this to clear the church debt after the renovations.'

Alex was relieved. 'I couldn't agree more Les. I'm so pleased we're on the same wavelength.'

'It was never in doubt. We're both big church men, and this will keep it going for years.' The two of them shook hands rigorously. 'What will happen to all this beautiful stuff now then?' Les asked.

'It will be going to the Museum of Liverpool and will be recorded as a find under the Portable Antiquities Scheme, and once they've finished, it should be returned to the church.'

'Well I hope they don't keep it in the church. This will have to be kept in secure storage surely,' said Les with concern.

'I agree.'

'And another thing,' continued Les. 'When it goes to the museum for evaluation, make sure you get a receipt.'

'I will for sure,' replied Alex.

Les turned to make his way out, then stopped and turned around. 'Alex, there's one other thing. You shouldn't be having any more problems with the nighthawks.'

'Oh, right. How come?'

'I've suspected one of our lads for a while. He's one of the farm labourers. I overheard a conversation about selling the stuff from Claybarn Field.'

'So, what did you do Les?'

'I challenged him, and told him his favourite toffee wrappers had been found in the excavations, and that I knew what he was up to. As soon as I mentioned the police he started to panic. Apparently, he's on some sort of probation with the threat of prison if he gets into more trouble. He'd been compromised and decided it was in his best interest to leave with immediate effect. Well, the immediate effect was my idea, so we won't be hearing from him again.'

'That's good news. But it's a bit sad that he has lost his job over it.'

'Well the way I look at it is that I can't afford to have anyone working for me who is dishonest, and he was.'

'I understand,' said Alex. 'There's another thing about Claybarn Field though. We've buried four old cow horns there that we believe are from the Civil War and could be loaded with black powder. You know … gunpowder. We think because the way that they were positioned around the safe, the idea was to blow the door off. Mind you, they would have needed twice as much just to leave a mark on the safe, but I guess they didn't know that at the time.

I'm going to ask the museum's advice or see if they will take them away.'

'Whereabouts in the field?' asked Les.

'At the top end, in line with your old Land Rover, and just beneath the hedge.'

'I'll make sure none of my lads goes into Claybarn, but I can't stop any dog walkers. They just please themselves.'

'I'll get it moved as soon as possible, and fill all the holes in as promised,' assured Alex.

'Thanks. Wait until Reverend Jill sees that lot,' Les said as he walked out, smiling and shaking his head.

I can't believe it was one of his own employees doing the nighthawking, Alex mused as Les left. *I wonder how much they've stolen or if any of it belongs to the church. I guess we'll never know.*

Alex walked back into the dining room and once again he was transfixed by the golden glow of the cross. *Absolutely impeccable, it really is.* He then looked at some of the other items of silverware. *The silver seems to be discolouring and tarnishing fast.*

It's probably due to the change of environment. They've probably been starved of oxygen for so long that when the air comes into contact with the sensitive surface, the metals reaction is exaggerated. I think I'll have another look at the safe.

Alex returned to the garage and knelt down to take a closer look at the safe, rubbing his finger across the surface. *Oxidation … hardly surprising. I'll go and call the finds liaison officer now.*

The response from the team at the Museum of Liverpool was as expected. They were sending someone over to take a look at the finds that afternoon, and they were contemplating what to do about the buried black powder finds still in Claybarn Field.

As Alex was considering making some tea, the rear door into the kitchen opened and Peter entered and asked, 'What sort of house are you running here?'

'What do you mean?'

'I found these two women loitering on your driveway,' Peter said with a big smile. He stepped aside to reveal Reverend Jill and the churchwarden Janice, each in turn giving Alex a big hug.

'Follow me and prepare to be amazed,' said Alex, as he walked them through to the dining room with Peter in tow.

When she saw the treasures, Jill cupped her hands to her face and the tears rolled down her cheeks. Janice just stood in amazement. Jill approached the cross, placed both hands upon it, closed her eyes and whispered a prayer.

Alex put his arm around Peter's shoulders. 'Let's give them a minute and put the kettle on,' he suggested.

'Dad, they're fantastic. And that gold cross ... it's got to be worth a fortune.'

'I think you're right son, and I hope it is.'

Later, over tea and biscuits, Alex suffered a barrage of questions, which he had expected. Jill posed the big one: 'I don't know how these things work. I presume it will get valued and sold, and you and Les take a percentage?'

'No,' said Alex. 'Les and I have already agreed that this all belongs to the church. It isn't ours. As far as we're concerned, we have no claim.'

Jill smiled, with a tear in her eye. 'We're all truly grateful.'

'Me included,' added Alex. 'It was an experience I'll never forget, opening that safe door. In fact, you must come and see the safe in the garage.'

He led them through and pointed to the hulk of a safe sitting in the middle of the garage floor. 'I don't know what it weighs Jill, but four men, planks and a rope were just enough,' Alex said, as he closed the door of the safe as slowly as he could. However, the door closed with a crash. 'What do you think of the writing on the front Jill? Or should I say, a series of overwritten letters. We think the letters are S, K, O, O, N, T.'

After only a few seconds, Jill said, 'Well, I think I know what this means. This safe is dedicated to the memory of St Oswald, King of Northumbria, so the actual letter order is S, T, O, K, O, N. He died in the seventh century, but some people still dedicate things to him today.'

'Well, you've just got yourself a safe,' said Alex. 'It's no longer a safe, mind, because it won't lock, but maybe it could be repaired.'

'I can't scrap it,' said Jill, 'not with the St Oswald dedication on its door. It will have to go back to the church vestry.'

'That's fine. Will you take it with you?' said Alex, and they all laughed.

After they had all returned to the dining room, Jill and Janice were looking at the documents that were laid out on the table.

'They're very fragile,' warned Alex. 'What I'd like to do is photograph each page. Don't worry though, I'll do it without flash, and it's much safer than photocopying. Then I can give them back to you Jill.'

'That's fine by me,' Jill replied. 'I'd like to put them back in the church safe in the vestry.'

'Okay,' agreed Alex. 'I can prepare them for you with acid-proof paper and acid-proof boxes. At least then you'll know they're not being neglected, because ultimately you'll want them to go to the county records office for safekeeping.'

'Yes, of course,' Jill replied. 'That's the right thing to do, and as long as we have copies of everything, they'll be useful for research and family history enquiries. I'm just going to take some photographs Alex, then we'll have to go. We have a deanery meeting to go to.'

'You as well Janice?' asked Alex.

'I'm afraid so,' Janice replied. 'A churchwarden's work is never done, but I've got to say, this is fantastic what you've found. This will be so good for the church, and as a committee we'll have to decide what we're going to do with it, and more importantly, where we're going to store it safely. It can't just go into the vestry safe.'

'I agree,' said Alex.

Jill and Janice left shortly afterwards; they were both quite emotional.

Later that afternoon Melissa Michaels, the finds liaison officer, and her assistant Matthew Rice, arrived from the Museum of Liverpool. They were shocked at the quality of the finds and the condition that they were in. They agreed that some sort of anaerobic conditions must have existed for the safe and its contents to remain in such good condition. Melissa wanted to take the items away that afternoon and had come equipped with storage boxes and packing.

When all the items were packed, excluding the old church documents, the required paperwork was completed and signed and a copy in the form of a receipt, listing all the items, was handed over to Alex.

'I'm just going to make a quick call to the Coroner,' said Melissa.

Peter looked a bit puzzled. Alex took him by the arm and walked him into the kitchen. 'Why the Coroner Dad?'

'It's okay,' Alex assured him. 'It seems a little strange, but under the Treasure Act it's a legal requirement to report it to the Coroner for your area. It's part of their role to administer such finds.'

Peter looked none the wiser. They walked back into the dining room just as Melissa was finishing her call: 'I'll send you the photographs and copies of all the documents. Yes, okay, speak to you later. Bye, bye.'

'Okay, all done,' Melissa explained to Alex and Peter. 'And I must say, this is by far the most valuable and interesting find I've been involved with, because of the unique designs, particularly on the chalices and ciboria, with their gorgeous red stones. We should hopefully be able to date the items and throw some light on their provenance. There'll be a lot of interest.'

'I have a few more items that will be of interest,' said Alex, as he handed over the musket rest, a cavalier stirrup, some musket balls, and two coins in a leather purse.

After a few seconds, Melissa said, 'Ah yes, classic Civil War era.' But it was Melissa's previous words that Alex was uneasy with: 'There will be a lot of interest.'

Melissa then asked, 'Can I just take a look at the safe please before I go? Then if you don't mind, if one of you can show Matt to the finds site to point out where these black powder flasks are. We're in two cars.'

'Okay,' agreed Alex. 'Peter, if you don't mind showing Matt.'

'No problem Dad.' Peter and Matt left for Claybarn Field.

Meanwhile, Alex showed Melissa the safe, pointing out that the writing on the door indicated that it belonged to St Oswald's church. She took some photographs of the safe and the old church documents before leaving. On the way out, Alex reminded her to 'look after the valuable cargo'.

Alex returned to the dining room, where all that was left were the old church documents and a receipt from the museum, and, of course, he still had a large lump of heavy metal on his garage floor.

Meanwhile, Peter had led Matt to Claybarn Field and discreetly shown him where the cow horn flasks had been buried. Matt had already made numerous telephone calls to his colleagues and other personnel at the museum, the result being that an army bomb disposal unit had been despatched, was on route, and expected to be there within two hours. Matt waited on site in his car, while Peter returned to his parents' house.

'Bomb disposal. Are you serious?' Alex asked Peter, as they sat in the dining room.

'That's what he said. He's consulted his boss and some other people, and they're on their way.'

'Well, it's their decision. They must believe it warrants that kind of response, but I doubt we'll see the flasks again.'

Whilst Peter had been at Claybarn Field with Matt, both Thomas and Derek had called Alex, wanting updates on the day's events. Alex took the opportunity to inform them about his conversation with Les and the sacking of the nighthawk. They were both pleased, as was Peter when Alex now told him.

'Anyway, I thought you weren't coming until this evening,' Alex said to his son.

'I wasn't. I just wanted to be here with my old man and his precious finds.'

'Er, less of the old, thank you.'

As they were talking, Karen walked into the kitchen. 'Hello,' she shouted.

'Hi,' said Peter, walking through to the kitchen to give his mum a hug.

'Why aren't you at work?' Karen asked him.

'Just a bit more time off. It's okay, it's owed to me. How are things at work for you Mum?'

'I love it, especially now it's part-time. The rest of my time I feel like I'm working for your dad on his treasure hunts.'

'You are,' shouted Alex from the dining room.

'In his dreams,' Karen said quietly to Peter.

Later that afternoon, Alex was passing by the rectory, where he saw Jill's car on the drive, so he decided to pull in for a quick word. He knocked on the door and Jill opened it almost immediately.

'Come in Alex. I've just made some tea, and would you like to try a slice of my lemon cake?'

'Jill, you know I love lemon cake. You don't need to ask.' Jill smiled and promptly returned with a tray on which there was a pot of tea, two cups and saucers, two plates and two thickly sliced pieces of lemon cake.

'How did your meeting go this afternoon?' asked Alex.

'Oh, it was okay. Usual thing these days – well it has been for several years – about diminishing attendances and growing costs. However, I had a nice feeling inside, and I think it was because I knew that our church was going to be saved, but sadly the chances are that one or two churches in this area are going to have to close, and very soon. In fact, we're still on the list of potential closures.'

'Did you or Janice mention the finds?' Alex asked.

'No, we thought it better not to until we know for sure it will all be returned to us.'

'I think that's wise. In fact, it was what I actually wanted to ask you to do, to keep it quiet at least until we've sorted out a secure storage place. As you say, it's best to wait until we get the items back, although I don't think it will be a problem. It's only a matter of time.

'I wanted to ask you about the other items that we found Jill. Along with musket balls there was a musket rest and a riding stirrup. I'd like to donate them to the church and put them on display in the historical area.'

'Oh, that would be lovely Alex. Thank you once again. I believe that we shouldn't hide away from the fact that we're on a battlefield site, and the church played such an instrumental part in the English Civil War for both sides.'

'Thanks Jill. When everything comes back from the museum, we can discuss things then. In fact, in all probability, they'll want us to collect the items from them.'

'Then I'll come with you to take possession of the items on behalf of the church, if you don't mind.'

'Not at all,' replied Alex. 'Actually, I was thinking that because we won't have any expensive items on display, we could perhaps get them copied on a 3D printer and display those. Then at least people would have an idea what the cherished church treasures look like.'

'I think that's a good idea too, as long as we don't start getting numerous break-ins because people are wanting to steal the real thing.'

'I think we'll have to make it perfectly clear,' said Alex, 'that the originals are not held in the church but at a secure location.'

The following day, Alex received a telephone call from Melissa at the museum, informing him that the cow horn flasks had been emptied of their explosive black powder contents and the flasks were now in their hands as part of the Claybarn find. Alex thought this was great news, as it only enhanced the find, and the church display would benefit.

Alex returned to Claybarn Field on numerous occasions over the next couple of weeks, firstly to make the field good after their excavations, then to continue metal detecting. He had no further interruptions from nighthawks.

He found a few musket balls but, on the whole, he didn't believe there was anything more to find in that field. Either that, or he was happy with what he had found. And who wouldn't be; it was, after all, the best find in years.

Things slowly returned to normal in the Helsby household, which was just as well because Louise was studying for her exams, and the excitement of the last couple of weeks was beginning to affect her concentration. The Tuesday Club had also now returned to its normal weekly outings.

Alex had contacted his old digging friend Dave, and they went to the local pub for a beer. In confidence, Alex told him all about the Claybarn Field finds. They spoke for hours, drank too much and, in the end, Dave had to stay over for the night. He had tried to get Alex to go on their latest dig, but Alex gave a legitimate excuse – the old favourite – his back. Pulling that safe out of the ground was the most pain he had ever felt, but the excitement and adrenalin had driven him forwards. Dave had left early the next morning after a call that Alex believed was from his wife. He had pencilled a note to Alex: 'Let's do it again soon', and left it on the kitchen worktop.

Alex decided to make a display case so that some of the finds could be displayed in the church. He had all the tools in his garage workshop, and he even had some nice beech timber that he could use for the case frame.

The old church safe had been pushed into a corner of the garage and was standing on its base, with its door pushed closed. *I don't know why, but I just have the feeling that the safe is going to be here for a long time*, Alex thought. *Jill knows there's nowhere for it to go.*

He decided to clean the garage up a little, using a stiff brush and shovel on the garage floor. For his bench worktop he had a small battery-operated handheld vacuum that fitted on to a charging bracket on the wall above the bench. The bench itself was two sideboards next to each other, but with one long plywood top. The whole unit was then screwed to the garage wall.

There was a small gap of about two centimetres between the two sideboards, because their tops were larger than their bases, causing a slight overhang. *That looks like a piece of paper that's fallen down the back. How am I going to get that out now?* The piece of paper was flat on the concrete block wall behind the bench and it was visible through the gap in the sideboards. *I need to try to slide it up, then grab it as it appears above the bench.*

Alex saw a long drill bit standing up against the wall. It was the drill bit he had used in Claybarn Field as a probe. *That should do the job.* He slotted the drill bit between the sideboards and rested the end on the wall just beneath the paper. Then raising the drill bit slowly, the paper was forced upwards and reappeared at the back of the bench. With his other hand, Alex grabbed it quickly before it slipped back down again.

He dropped the drill bit to look at the piece of paper. *This is the blank piece of paper that the church documents were in.* He was just about to screw the paper up and bin it, but for some strange reason decided to hold it up to the light. He couldn't see any writing. *Looks like a very faint pattern though. I could be mistaken.*

It reminded Alex of something he had read about clandestine correspondence in *The Autobiography of a Hunted Priest.* It was how Father John Gerard communicated with the outside world when he was locked up in the Tower of London. He wrote secret messages between the lines of an ordinary letter, but he used orange juice as ink, as it's more or less impossible to see, but when heated up, the orange ink writing darkens.

Alex took the piece of paper up to his study to look at it under his illuminating magnifying glass. *I can't really tell if it's writing or not. I know that in Father Gerard's book he mentions about holding the paper over a naked flame, such as a candle, to reveal what's written. I think I'll try something different.*

He was still unsure whether the paper contained any writing, but he needed to find out. He went down into the kitchen and turned on the oven, placed the paper on the top shelf, and waited for what seemed like an eternity but was only about ten minutes. He opened the oven, pulled out the paper quickly and placed it on the kitchen worktop. To his amazement, there was what looked like a full page of longhand writing. It was extravagant, with its large curly capitals and intricacies. *I don't believe this. I've found a secret letter. I must photograph it now in case it deteriorates and loses its wording. I can't believe it; I can't wait to read it.*

Alex's hands were shaking as he grabbed his camera and took multiple photographs. He then plugged the camera into his laptop to upload them. Once the photographs were on the screen, he was able to enhance them using some software. He could darken the letters and intensify them to make them easier to read. After doing this, he stared at the screen in astonishment.

To whose concern it may be.

The monetary treasures of the church I leave intact, but there are further rewards that I believe will be significant. As such, the efforts by myself to conceal the papers have been considerable and time-consuming, although this letter I am afraid was written in haste.

I have secreted a quantity of important papers from previous and trusted benefactors within the church of St Oswald. My reasons for this I make clear:
... The church is in a poor state of repair.
... There is fear of looting by the armies of the Civil War.

It is therefore not safe to leave the documents either in the church or in the care of the rectory. As I journey much to London with the Westminster assembly, and due to the quantity of papers involved, I am unable to keep them in person. The resting place of which is disclosed within the content of this letter.

I trust, therefore, that the recipient will be an honest-living, righteous man of the church, who will take the utmost in care and respect of these papers, some of which have been deposited in the custody of St Oswald's for many years.

Your   most   humble   servant
Charles Herle   8 August 1648

Alex was stunned. *I really can't believe this is happening to me. The Claybarn find isn't finished yet, far from it. This is going to be a puzzle. He doesn't say where the papers are, other than their final resting place is disclosed within the content of the letter. Perhaps it's some kind of code or cipher.*

He picked up the letter and once again scrutinised every word. He turned the letter over. It was totally blank on the reverse. Turning it back to the front he looked for any hidden words or phrases, or any marks or signs. There was nothing other than the light-brown wording.

He placed the letter in a large brown envelope, picked up a roll of adhesive labels, and wrote 'THE SANCTUARY CIPHER' on one of them in a black felt pen. He then peeled the label off and stuck it to the front of the brown envelope, placing the envelope into a box file standing on his desk. Suddenly, he heard the kitchen door being opened and Karen shouting, 'It's only me.'

'I'm in the study,' shouted Alex. 'I've got something that I think you'll want to see.'

'Now there's an offer I can't refuse,' was the reply from the kitchen. Karen joined Alex in the study.

'Right, do you remember when we pulled the documents out of the safe?' Alex asked.

'Yes, it was only a few weeks ago,' Karen replied sarcastically.

'The documents were in a fold of paper, just to keep them together,' Alex continued.

'Yes ... and?'

'Well, that fold of paper had fallen down the back of my bench in the garage.'

'Okay, but I thought it was just plain paper.'

'Yes, so did I, or at least I did until I looked at it closely. I thought I could see lines or letters very faintly, then it came to mind about Father John Gerard and his invisible orange juice ink writing, which was supposed to have aided his escape from the Tower. With this being from the same era, I thought that there was a good possibility, so I erm ...'

'What?'

'I put it in the oven ... and it worked.' Alex leaned over and pulled the envelope out from the box file, gently revealing the sheet of paper from within.

'Oh my god,' exclaimed Karen, staring at the sheet of paper. 'It's a little difficult to read.'

'I know, but look at this.' Alex pressed a button on the keypad of the laptop, and there in all its glory was a shot of the sheet of paper, the contents of which showed a perfectly legible letter.

Karen gasped, sat down, and started to read. 'This is fantastic. So, somewhere in this letter is a clue leading to the hidden papers in the church.'

'That's right,' said Alex. 'The sanctuary cipher. Well, that's what I'm calling it.'

Karen looked at Alex. 'You clever man, you.' She stood up and hugged him, then kissed him on the lips.

'I'll feel clever if we can find these papers,' Alex said.

'We?'

'Yes, we … team Helsby,' confirmed Alex. He then printed off a couple of copies of the letter. 'I'll go and make some tea while you get changed.'

'Okay, thanks.'

A short while later they were both on the sofa in the lounge scrutinising their own copy of the letter.

Karen looked up and said, 'Considering he said he wrote it in haste, he has made a pretty good job of it. The lettering is so concise, and when you think about it, he wouldn't have been able to see what he was writing. He was just going on instinct, and is naturally a good neat writer. Who is he anyway?'

'He was the rector of St Oswald's at the time of the Civil War. In fact, he was the incumbent for many years, and if my memory serves me correctly, it was because of his friendship with the Stanley family and the Earl of Derby that he became rector of St Oswald's in 1626.

'He was rector until the early 1650s. He died and was buried in the church in 1659. He had a full, active and political life, which is surprising for a man of the cloth. He was also an author and published many religious pamphlets. He moved in very high places.'

'What do you think the papers will be about?'

'He mentions in the letter about a quantity of important papers from previous and trusted benefactors. Under normal circumstances, a benefactor is a person who gives financial help, like a sponsor, so I guess the papers could be financial, or it could be anything that the benefactor wanted to leave in the safe. The rector may have felt obliged to say yes.'

Karen, looking a bit perplexed, said, 'He says that the resting place of the papers is disclosed within the content of this letter. But presumably because he doesn't actually give the location, it must be hidden within the words. Now I see why the brown envelope had the sanctuary cipher written on the front. Can I have another look at the original Alex?'

'Okay.' Alex got up from the sofa and made his way to the study. He picked up the brown envelope and returned to the sofa, sliding the letter out of the envelope. *It looks like it may have faded, or is it because we've been looking at enhanced copies?* He handed the letter to Karen, who immediately held it up to the light.

She turned to Alex. 'You took a gamble, didn't you?'

'What do you mean?'

'You took a gamble putting this valuable historic document in the oven.'

Alex looked at Karen, and unusually seemed lost for words, stuttering, 'Well … er … yes, you're right, but it was an educated gamble, and as far as anyone else is concerned it was just a blank piece of paper.'

'Alex, you know that if that had been sent to a lab, they would have revealed the contents of the letter.'

'I'm sure,' said Alex. 'But it had been lost behind my work bench and I fortuitously came across it only today.'

Karen smiled. 'You know what you are? A slippery character.'

'I don't think that's fair. Maybe a little over-enthusiastic.'

'So, what do we do now?' asked Karen. 'Start ripping the church to pieces?'

'Of course not. We must crack the sanctuary cipher … then we rip the church to pieces,' Alex said, winking at his wife.

'Has anyone else seen this letter?'

'No.'

'Then except for Jill and Janice, that's how it should remain, don't you think?' Karen suggested.

'Yes, I think you're right. No one else needs to know, otherwise people will be bashing the door down and putting the church at risk. We have to find these missing papers though, sooner rather than later. So, let's read this letter and see what theories we can come up with.'

That afternoon, the pair of them sat together and attempted to decipher what it was they were looking for. And there lay the problem: they didn't know whether they were looking for a word, a phrase, a code or something else.

That evening, Jill came to the Helsby's and Alex fully explained his actions and his findings. He gave Jill a copy of the enhanced letter, and she agreed that it shouldn't become common knowledge, and should remain between the three of them and Janice, until hopefully at some point when the papers were found, and a further decision could be made.

After Jill had gone, Alex was in the study looking at the letter on his laptop screen. *Karen was right. Considering he stated he wrote the letter in haste it doesn't seem to be rushed. The resting place of which is disclosed within the content of this letter ... what does he mean? Where is it? I can't see it in the content. I'll have to start looking at every word to see if I can form a sentence from the starting letter of each word, or the ending letter of each word. Maybe I'm not looking for a sentence; maybe just a code or a cipher or ... this is going to drive me mad, but somewhere in that church are valuable hidden papers. I'll go in the morning while the church is empty and just have a nosey around. I don't know where I'll look. I never thought I'd be doing this in our sacred church but, according to Charles Herle, the rewards will be significant. But to whom, the finder or the church?*

That night, Karen and Alex went to bed early, each reading their own copy of the letter. The bedroom was silent as they both scribbled away on notepads, each carrying out their own method of extracting whatever it was they were looking for. It wasn't long before they were both sound asleep.

Chapter 12

Decoding the Cipher

THE FOLLOWING morning, Karen was up early and out to her morning shift at the museum in Warrington. Alex wasn't aware, but Karen had taken her copy of the letter with her and had every intention of asking for her colleague's help. This was contrary to her discussion with Alex the previous night about keeping the letter confidential, but her colleague Angelica, known as Angel, was particularly good with documents and was a well-respected expert in palaeography. She could transcribe old English documents and was particularly good at modern-day explanations of the historic written word and terminology.

It was just before lunchtime that Karen took the opportunity to seek out Angel, who was in what was known as the book depository, down in the basement.

Karen was carrying the copy of the letter in an envelope when she heard Angel's voice from the far end of the room. 'Is that envelope for me?'

'Well actually, yes, it is,' replied Karen, walking up to a desk that was heavily laden with books. Angel was sitting behind the desk and as usual had a pen stuck inside a bun on the top of her head. 'Angel, there's something I've been wanting to ask you for quite a while.'

'Okay, fire away.'

'Is that pen in your hair to hold your bun together or is just somewhere to keep it?' Angel smiled and pulled out the pen. Almost immediately her hair fell down to shoulder length. It was very straight and very dark, and as it fell across her face it seemed to reduce her from a forty-year-old woman approaching her middle age to a woman just into her thirties. She was very attractive. Within a few seconds Angel had rolled up her hair back into a bun and thrust the pen through the centre, almost like a magic trick.

'Does that answer your question?' Angel said.

Karen was impressed with the efficiency and speed of hand that Angel had shown. 'How did you learn that?' she asked.

'Gymnastics is to blame. My hair always had to be up and away from the face. My mum always did it for me, and as I got older and into my teens, she told me I had to do it myself, so I've done it ever since. Anyway, enough about me. What can I do for you?'

Karen then explained the letter, the confidentiality aspect, and the fact that, so far, they had been unable to identify the resting place that was supposed to be disclosed within the letter.

Angel seemed to physically grow as she read the letter; her back straightened and her manicured eyebrows lifted in a kind of surprised expression. 'Well, it certainly looks like the real deal, even though this is a copy. It would be much better if I could see the original though,' Angel suggested.

'That's a bit tricky at the moment. I don't think Alex would be too impressed if he knew I'd shown you the copy, never mind the real thing. I agreed to keep it confidential.'

'Okay, mum's the word, but if you change your minds there's usually more to glean from an original document. I wonder what the important papers are. This letter seems to insinuate that you as the finder may have already retrieved the monetary treasures.'

'I can't say any more,' said Karen, smiling.

Angel put her hand to her open mouth in a shocked sort of way then rubbed her hands together and asked, 'Can you leave this letter with me for this afternoon to give me chance to look at it properly?'

'Of course. I'll collect it from you in the morning. And thank you.' Karen leaned over and gave Angel a short hug.

******

Alex was in the study on his laptop, having just returned from spending the last couple of hours in church looking in areas where he hadn't previously looked, but he was no further on. He was reading the letter on the screen yet again when the telephone landline rang. He picked up the handset from its cradle.

'Hello. Is that Mr Helsby?' the caller asked.

'It is.'

'Hello. This is Detective Constable Tony Andretti here from Cheshire Police. Would it be possible for me to call to see you this afternoon?'

'Oh, er, what about?' asked Alex, nervously.

'It's okay, it's about the Coroner's report. I believe you've had an interesting find.'

Alex was anxious for the rest of the afternoon. *If the police know about the Claybarn find, bang goes confidentiality. I just never thought that the report via the Coroner would end up with the police being notified. I guess it makes sense really. They're looking to see whether there's been an offence committed.*

Maybe there was, over three hundred and fifty years ago. I'd like to see how they investigate that.

Soon after, the kitchen door opened. Karen was back with a pile of groceries, which she called the weekly shop, although she seemed to end up in the supermarket every other day, buying more groceries.

Alex joined her in the kitchen. 'How are you?' he asked.

'I'm fine,' said Karen. 'Have you had any joy? Or should I say have you cracked the sanctuary cipher?'

'Afraid not, and I've just had a call from Cheshire Police. They're on the way to speak to me about the find.'

'Oh, right. And how did they get to find out about it?'

'Through the Coroner's Office report.'

'Well, make sure that you tell them not to release it to the press bureau,' warned Karen.

'I tell you what, you can ask them yourself. I've just seen a car pull up outside.'

Detective Constable Tony Andretti and his colleague wanted to know the circumstances of the find. They already had photocopies of the items, and once they realised there was no evidence of a crime being committed and that all the goods were going to be returned to their rightful owner, St Oswald's Church, they seemed to switch off and become more casual in their attitude.

That's when Karen asked them not to release any information to the press bureau. Andretti agreed, particularly since there was no evidence of a crime involved. It wasn't really their information to release. The detectives left, offering their congratulations for the Claybarn find.

Later that afternoon Karen's mobile rang while she and Alex were in the study. It was Angel. Karen got up and left the room to take the call. Alex got up and walked across the study. Karen was only on the other side of the door, so he was well within earshot of the conversation, as Karen unwittingly had her mobile on speakerphone.

'Did you find anything in the letter?' Karen asked Angel.

'Well no, actually, I didn't. I've had a close look under the magnifier but there doesn't seem to be anything hidden. However, reading the letter numerous times, I can't help thinking that the writer may be trying to say that physically the resting place is disclosed within the letter. If you consider the letter an open envelope, then the clue may rest within any document associated with it. Were there any other documents with it Karen?'

'Yes, there were. The letter was folded over a wad of documents, keeping them together.'

'Then I suggest that you look at those documents. They could give you the key to the resting place that you're looking for.'

'We're so grateful for your help. Thank you for this.'

'No problem,' Angel replied. 'I'll see you in the morning.'

'Bye Angel.'

Karen rang off and went back into the study, where Alex was back in his seat at the desk. 'Who was that love?' he asked.

'Oh, it was Angel from the museum. It was work stuff.'

'Then how come you were talking about the letter?'

Karen looked really annoyed. 'Were you listening to me? That was a private conversation,' she said, her voice increasing in volume.

'It wasn't that private. I could hear all of it because you were on speakerphone. We agreed to keep this quiet for the time being Karen. I can't believe you've gone behind my back.'

'Oh, don't be so dramatic.'

'Karen, we agreed.'

Karen's voice rose again. 'Well I thought we needed help. She's trustworthy and honest for god's sake.'

'She'd better be.'

At this, Karen turned away, and on her way out of the room, said, 'If that's your attitude, you can do all your own research from now on.' She slammed the door shut so hard that a calendar that was pinned to the back of it fell to the floor.'

Alex just sat there, annoyed with himself for not handling the situation better. *I don't see why she's asked for help. Why couldn't she just keep quiet? I know I'm going to get the silent treatment for a while, so I may as well ask her.*

Alex walked into the lounge, where Karen was sitting on the sofa reading what looked like an old reference book on the history of Warrington. 'Why did you tell this, what's her name, Angel, about the letter?' Alex asked her.

'Because we need the help.'

'How do we know she isn't going to tell the world about the letter? And I presume that you've told her about the find.'

'Well no, not exactly. I haven't told her what we've found, but she knows we've found something.'

'Great,' said Alex sarcastically, but he could tell that Karen was becoming annoyed again.

'I'd trust her with my life,' Karen assured him. 'If there was ever any doubt, I wouldn't have told her a thing, and it's a shame that you think so little of me after all these years of marriage.' She got up to walk out of the room, but Alex gently took hold of her arm and pulled her towards him. Karen glared at him and said, 'Just remember, I'm your wife, not your employee, and sometimes I feel that ...'

Alex interrupted her. 'I'm sorry. I know. I just wanted to keep everything low-key. It's our little project that I want us to work on together.'

'I understand that, but there are going to be times when we need other people's input, and I believe this is one of them.'

'Okay,' Alex said, and wrapped his arms around her in a vice-like grip. 'Just don't let it happen again.'

'You sod,' Karen shouted, and Alex knew that her right leg had been bent and her knee was strategically positioned to attack the area that hurts the most.

'I'm joking,' Alex pleaded. 'Please, let's work together as team Helsby again.' He could feel Karen relax in his arms, then she placed her arms around him, and they embraced.

'I haven't told you what she said,' Karen said, excitedly.

'Who?'

'Angel. She thinks that the line that states "is enclosed within the content of this letter" may be more metaphoric.'

'In what way?'

'Well, once I explained to her about the other documents that were with the letter, she thought that the letter may be saying that the resting place could be within the documents and not necessarily the letter, because of the way in which the letter was folded around the documents.'

'That's not good news Karen. There are burial, baptism and marriage records, as well as several other documents. Some are quite old and in a poor state, so how on earth are we going to be able to make any sense out of that lot, never mind find a clue? This is a huge job. I need a structure on how to approach this. I'm just going up to the study. I've got some thinking to do.'

'Okay,' replied Karen. 'I've just got to nip out, but I'll give you a hand when I get back.'

'Okay,' said Alex, already on his way to the study.

Meanwhile, in Cheshire Police CID office, Tony Andretti was openly speaking about the riches of the Claybarn find in the presence of police officers and civilian staff alike.

******

Later, in his study, Alex had all of the documents they had found in the safe on his desk. There was a sheet from a large flip-board pad pinned to the wall. Alex had written on the sheet with a marker pen:

Record the following:
– any references to a location within the church

– if yes, type of document, page and line
number
– any errors, omissions or additions
– any underlining or other highlighting of
a particular word or phrase
– any possible hidden words or phrases
(orange juice ink)

Alex was deep in thought. *I hope Angel is right about this, but there's only one way to find out.* He picked up one set of documents that were held together in the corner by a piece of string threaded through every page, similar to a modern-day treasury tag. The front page said 'St Oswald's, Winwick, burial records 1599–1620.

As he turned the page, he was faced with a series of neatly ruled columns providing information on the date of the burial, the name of the person buried, the age of the person, a plot reference number and the signature of the official making the entry. He was able to skim through these quickly by referring to the plot reference column to see if any were buried within the church itself rather than the churchyard.

He drew a blank on this search, as there were no internal burials during this period.

He then returned to the opening page and searched for any other anomalies. Searching under his magnifier, nothing stood out, and he couldn't see any of the telltale signs of orange juice ink.

It took him approximately an hour to go through this set of documents to his satisfaction, and apart from a couple of word changes and corrections, there was nothing to indicate anything out of the ordinary.

The next set of documents were the baptism records 1610–1625, laid out in a similar fashion with columned pages. He skipped over each page, looking for reference to any part of the church. Again, this proved negative. There were several errors and corrections but nothing that jumped out. There were also no traces of orange juice ink on any of the pages.

This series of documents took Alex considerably longer, in fact it was early evening and Karen was shouting for him to come down for his evening meal. *Where has the last couple of hours gone? It seems as if I've only been in my study for ten minutes. This search is captivating and all-absorbing, but I think I'll leave it for tonight and watch some television.*

It ended up being a nice quiet evening, the only disruption being a telephone call from Reverend Jill, just to ask whether they had heard anything from the museum. Alex said that he hadn't, and told Jill that it usually takes about four weeks, but that he would call them in the morning.

Alex went to bed early that evening, but was unable to settle. At 1 a.m. he decided to get up. He went down into the kitchen and made a cup of tea, then he made the fatal mistake of going to his study.

He started looking at the third set of documents, which were some kind of record of the marriages that took place in the church. These were very vague, of random dates and, to top it all, these documents appeared to have incurred some kind of water damage before they were buried in the safe. *I may as well make a start on these, seeing as I'm up.*

It was noticeable that a lot of these documents had a waterline across the middle, and everything below this had been erased or obscured. *These look like they've been sitting half soaked in water for a long time before being rescued and lumped together with all these other documents.*

Amongst the other papers there was information relating to numbers of attendees at services, and names of recusants, who were people of the Roman Catholic faith that refused to attend Church of England services and therefore committed a statutory offence. These documents were quite revealing and gave an insight into the issues of the day and some of the reasons that people gave for not going to church on a Sunday.

Before Alex knew it, the sky was getting lighter. It was now past 6 a.m. and he had been in his study for another five hours. He was dog-tired and made his way to bed, slipping under the duvet next to Karen and falling asleep immediately.

Karen was up at 8 a.m. and woke Alex just half an hour later, before she went off to work. He wasn't impressed, but it wasn't her fault; she didn't know that he had been up for most of the night in his study.

He lay in bed thinking about what he had found out so far. *This thing is taking over me. I've become obsessed. All I can think about is this missing location, supposedly contained within the contents of a letter or numerous other documents. But if Charles Herle had written the letter in haste as he said he had, surely he wouldn't have had the time or opportunity to incorporate the clue within a whole series of documents. I'm still not sure that Angel is right.*

Alex got out of bed and went to his study. This time, instead of looking at the scanned image of the letter on his laptop screen, he took the original document out of its file. *Come on, it's got to be in this letter.* He placed it under his illuminated magnifier and searched and searched and searched every millimetre of the page, but still nothing jumped out at him. *There's something I'm not seeing here.*

After showering and having a light breakfast of toast and jam, Alex was on the telephone to Karen. 'Hi, its only me,' he said. 'I was thinking ... do you think your friend Angel would have another look at the letter?'

'I'll ask her.'

'Do you have a microscope there?'

'Yes, there's one in the lab. Why?'

'Well, I'd like her to have another look at the original letter, but through a microscope this time,' Alex suggested.

'I'm sure she's already done that. What exactly are you looking for that she hasn't already looked for?'

'Nothing new. Exactly the same, but I just want her to have another, closer look.'

'Well, I can only ask,' said Karen.

'It's just that I'm sure there's something there that we've missed.'

'You mean that she's missed.'

'No not at all. I just have a feeling that the clue is in the letter and all these other documents are just sending us off on a wild-goose chase.'

'Okay, I'll ask her.'

'Great. I'll bring the original letter in this morning,' said Alex.

'What, so soon? Before I've asked her? That's very persistent of you.'

'I know,' said Alex, 'but I'm in a persistent kind of mood.'

Later that morning, Alex arrived at the museum and Karen came to meet him in the entrance area. He handed over the letter in a brown envelope. 'Look after it,' he said.

'This is a museum. We do have a habit of looking after things here.'

'I know. I just can't help myself.'

'Do you not think you're getting a bit obsessed by all of this?'

'Well, I just want to see it through to its conclusion. But yes, it is taking over a bit, and I'm sorry if I've been a bit well er ...'

'Bullish,' Karen finished his sentence for him.

'Yes, okay, bullish, whatever that means.'

'I'll take this to Angel now. I'm sure that she will look at it as soon as she can.'

'Okay. Thanks.'

'Where are you off to now?' Karen asked him.

'Home. I've got some calls to make.'

'Can you vacuum out the study. It's a disgrace in there.'

'Yes, I know, and yes, I will.'

They hugged briefly before going their separate ways.

Back at home in his study, Alex was looking at the letter on his laptop screen. *There's something here. It's screaming out at me, but I can't see it*. He went downstairs to the kitchen to make an instant coffee.

Sitting on one of the stools adjacent to the worktop, he picked up an orange from the fruit bowl. When he went over to the fridge for milk, he noticed that one of the egg sections in the fridge contained a lemon, so he took the lemon out of the fridge and placed it alongside the orange on the worktop. *I wonder … I should have tried this before now.*

He cut the lemon and the orange in half and squeezed the juice out of each into two saucers. He then returned to his study carrying the two saucers of juice and placed them on his desk. From the top drawer of the desk, he took an old fountain pen that his father had given him before he died. This was the type of pen that didn't use cartridges, but was filled from a bottle of ink by inserting the nib into the fluid and pulling up on the syringe to draw the ink into its body. The pen had been cleaned and flushed through with clear water many years ago and then just left in the drawer.

Alex dipped the nib of the pen into the lemon juice and wrote the number 8 on a piece of paper, then cleaned the nib and drew some water through to clean it. He then dipped it into the orange juice and wrote the number 8 again, so the two were next to each other on the paper. Allowing the juice to dry to almost invisible, Alex then took the paper back downstairs and placed it in the oven, turned on the heat, then sat on the stool and watched the paper through the glass door.

After about ten minutes he noticed that the paper was losing its shape, so he opened the oven and pulled out the paper, placing it quickly on the worktop. The two numbers he had written could be seen as clear as day. After turning off the oven, Alex returned to the study with the paper.

On his desk in the study, under his illuminating magnifying glass, he could see a colour variation between the two numbers. The orange juice number had darkened slightly more. He then scanned the paper into his laptop and looked at the image on the screen. He could see no difference in the numbers – in colour, density or clarity – proving that the scanning process isn't a wholly accurate representation of the original. *Charles Herle could have deliberately written the letter in different juices, in effect hiding a code within the content. It's a long shot, but it's got to be worth looking at.*

Alex picked up his mobile and called Karen, explaining to her his findings, and asking whether Angel could look specifically for deviations in the colours of the lettering.

Within the hour his mobile phone rang, and he didn't recognise the number, so he wasn't going to pick up. *Could be someone from the Liverpool museum though, with an update on the Claybarn find.* He decided to answer. 'Hello, Alex Helsby.'

'Hi Alex, its Angel here about your letter.'

'Angel, thanks for calling, and thanks for the time spent working on this. I hope it's not going to get you into any trouble with the hierarchy.'

'No, not at all. I thought I'd better call you to let you know that I've found something in the letter.'

'Fantastic. Please fire away,' Alex said, with excitement.

'I've been looking at the colouring of the letters, and there's a definite use of another fluid. In fact, it's used on only five occasions within the whole letter, and the five occasions occur in the sentence "the resting place of which is disclosed within the content of this letter."'

'I don't believe it,' exclaimed Alex. 'It's too good to be true. Which letters are they?'

'The "t" in the, followed by the "n" in resting, followed by the "w" in which, then the "c" in disclosed, and finally the "f" of the word of, which gives you TNWCF. Does this mean anything to you Alex?'

'No, but I'll be working on it until it does. Angel, I can't thank you enough.'

'It's a pleasure. It's really interesting working on something different for a change. Any time you think I can be of use, please give me a call.'

'Thank you again, and yes I will. Bye for now.'

'Goodbye,' Angel replied.

Alex was looking at the note he had written on the writing pad. TNWCF. He couldn't stop smiling. *If I was leaving a code for someone that led to a location in a large building, how would I do it? I think I can crack this. Five letter coordinates relating to somewhere within the church. Think Alex, think. Charles Herle was rector of St Oswald's in 1626 and he died in 1659. The earliest parts of the church are the tower and the Legh Chapel, which were built in the mid thirteen hundreds. The nave and the Gerard Chapel came later, then much later the chancel is Victorian. This rules out certain parts of the church, although they could have been there previously under a different guise.*

Alex pulled out a small plan of the church that he kept in one of the set of document drawers in the study. It was a hand-drawn plan with an age to each section of the building written in capitals. *TNWCF. I wonder whether they're in the correct order or scrambled? If they're in the correct order, I can see* two potential coordinates already – north-west, so could the 'c' mean corner, and could the 'f' mean font?

Alex decided that he could rule out the font, because there had never been one in the north-west corner. *Could it be tower north-west corner? If it was tower north-west corner floor, that could work, although under the floor of a medieval and damp tower wouldn't be the best location to keep documents.*

Alex took a break and called Jill to arrange to meet and inform her about his findings. *I'll need to see Janice as well. It's only right to keep the churchwarden up to speed.* He was beside himself; he was super-excited, like a small child with a new toy. *Tower north-west corner floor, tower north-west corner floor, tower north-west corner floor*, went over and over in his head.

Alex called Jill but there was no reply, so he called Janice and agreed to go round to her house immediately, as she was planning an outing to the shops. He took a copy of the letter, locked the house, jumped into the SUV, and ten minutes later arrived at Janice's house. *I'm sure that's Jill's car. Janice never said she was here.*

He walked up the path and knocked on the door. Janice opened the door and welcomed him. 'Please come in. I have another visitor.'

Alex walked into the lounge, where Jill was sitting with a pile of papers on her knees. 'Good morning Jill. How are you?' he asked.

'Very well thank you.'

'I'm pleased you're here,' said Alex. 'There are a few things I'd like to discuss ... a few more developments.' He then explained the blank sheet of paper that wasn't blank, the fact that he had cooked it in the oven to reveal the hidden message, then Karen's involvement and Angel's contribution in revealing the hidden cipher.

Alex went on to explain that the five of them were the only people who knew about the letter and that's how he would like to keep it. Jill agreed that the confidential aspect had to be of the utmost importance, but both her and Janice were concerned about the need for a faculty to have any works carried out in the church and that the diocese was understandably liable to refuse any works that involved digging, removing, drilling, fixing, and definitely any excavations. However, Alex could tell that she was excited by the prospect of finding more treasures in the form of valuable documents. He knew that her passion for history was as strong as his.

When Alex explained his theory on 'TNWCF', the three of them agreed to make a quick visit to the church. Alex drove the short distance; Janice unlocked the church and they headed in the direction of the tower. Entering through the vestry door they stepped down a level into the nave and then down a couple of steps into the bell tower, the bell ringers' domain.

Alex walked over to the north-west corner and pointed at the floor. He was pointing at a large stone paving slab, probably about one-metre square in size. The slab was broken in the centre and the cracks fanned out to the edges, effectively quartering it.

'So, you think this is the spot?' asked Jill.

'I think this is a possibility. Tower north-west corner floor,' said Alex.

Janice spoke up: 'We won't be able to take that up without a faculty, and even if they said yes, they would want to know why. Then the confidentiality aspect would be gone.'

'Okay, let's leave it there for now,' suggested Jill, giving Alex a sideward glance. He had seen this look before, and knew she was on his side, but that she just needed to have a quiet word with Janice.

'If you could take us back now Alex,' Jill added. 'I need to be on my way. I'm giving communion in the nursing home in thirty minutes.'

'Sure, no problem.' Alex dropped them off at Janice's then made his way back to the church to take another look. He parked in the church car park and made his way up the footpath, turning right, in the direction of the tower. *I think I'll just look around the outside of the north-west corner of the tower. I don't know why.*

There was a row of burial stones laid flat around the tower walls, then there were two single wooden doors, which were used by the bell ringers only. These were secured by a padlock, which was always left open whenever people were actually in the church, in case of fire, as it was another means of fire exit. *These burial stones were probably put here in the seventies when the churchyard was reordered.*

Alex decided to take another look inside. He had a spare vestry key so made his entrance through its door, then made his way down to the tower, where he stood in front of the broken paving slab. *Why on earth would anyone hide anything under there? It just doesn't make sense. It's probably damp too. I wonder how the slab got broken like that.*

Kneeling down, Alex ran his hands along the cracks and noticed that they were emanating from a small circular hole in the centre of the slab. He used his index finger to feel around the edge of the hole. *It's very circular and smooth. It feels man-made.*

Knowing there was nothing more he could do, Alex left the church, walked to his car, then made his way home. Karen had just pulled on to the drive when he arrived, so he pulled in alongside her. She unlocked the front door and held it open for him.

'How is my clever husband then? You were right.' She pecked him on the cheek. They went through into the kitchen and Karen filled the kettle. 'Does the cipher mean anything to you?' she asked.

'Yes, I think so. I think it means tower north-west corner floor. I've been in the church with Jill and Janice.'

'And what did they think?'

'Jill seemed … well … a bit hard to read. And Janice was too worried about having to get a faculty.'

'I'm surprised at Jill. She's usually a no-nonsense woman who gets things done.'

'I know,' agreed Alex, 'but it's a little bit sensitive, and technically there should be a faculty from the diocese.'

'But what do you want to do? You're not going to open up a trench in the tower, are you? It's ridiculous.'

'No. There's a stone paving slab in the corner that's broken, and I know it seems unlikely, but the slab has had a hole drilled in its centre, maybe when it was originally laid. It could have had a pull ring to enable it to be lifted.'

'Well we're not going to give up on this are we,' said a defiant Karen. 'I've a good mind to call Jill.'

'No. There's no need, and it won't do any good. We'll just have to leave it with her. I'm sure she'll get back to us soon.'

The following evening there was a knock at Alex and Karen's door. Karen answered; it was Jill. 'Hi Jill. Please come in. How are you doing?'

'I'm very well Karen, thank you. I hope I'm not disturbing you.'

'No, of course not, please come through. Alex is in the lounge.'

Alex was as always pleased to see Jill. They had a good relationship and liked each other's company. *I hope she's here to talk about the letter, and I hope it's good news.*

Jill sat down on the sofa and Karen offered her some tea, which she accepted. 'How is Louise doing? I haven't seen her in a while,' said Jill.

'No, neither have we,' replied Alex. 'She spends most of her time in her bedroom revising for her exams. Or at least that's what she says she's doing.'

'Oh, I'm sure she is. She's very conscientious.'

'I'll call her down,' Alex suggested.

'Oh no, please leave her. I'll catch up with her again. Maybe when she's finished all her studying.'

'She would like that,' said Alex, as Karen came into the room with a tray of tea and biscuits.

'I just wanted to say that what you've done for the church over the last couple of weeks is greatly appreciated,' Jill said, 'and if all the finds you've made come back to where they belong, it's safe to say that the church will be financially secure for many years to come. Many an unscrupulous person would have taken it for themselves, but thank goodness you and Karen are people of the church.'

'Thanks Jill,' said Karen, and Alex smiled in appreciation of Jill's comments.

Jill returned the smile, and continued: 'But the real reason I'm here is to talk about your letter and your theory about hidden documents below the floor in the tower. I've had a long conversation with Janice about this, and as you know she only has the church interests at heart and doesn't want to fall foul of the diocese.

'We do, however, think that the paving slab in question is a trip hazard, particularly for the bell ringers, and we were wondering whether you could take it up, level it and refit it. Then if you could put it back down more or less the same, but level. We don't see a requirement for a faculty.

'Now I understand this may mean disturbing some of the material below the slab, but there's no record of there ever being any interments in that area of the tower, but we still feel that the work should be carried out covertly, and at a time when no one is likely to enter the church to replace flowers, attend choir practice or bell-ringing practice, or for any other reason. I think it would be much easier to handle if we keep this amongst ourselves.'

Thank goodness. I just hope that I'm right. Alex felt a wave of relief wash over him. 'I agree, and I'm fine with that. It won't do any harm in looking at what lies beneath and at the same time correcting a health and safety hazard. When would be the best day to do it? Or should I say night?'

'I think a Friday and Saturday are the best nights, so I'll just leave you to it and wish you every success,' said Jill.

'Thanks Jill. I think this Friday is the best option, and I'm looking forward to it. I'll keep you informed.'

'Okay, that's fine. And just another thing,' added Jill, 'don't park your car in the church car park. Someone will see it or see you going in or out and then the cat will be out of the bag. People will be ringing me at all hours wanting to know what's going on in the church.'

Jill left after two cups of tea and two slices of cake. Alex and Karen were happy that they were being allowed to put their theory to the test, compliments to Jill and her persuasive case put forward to Janice.

'I'm not sure I'm keen on working in a church in the evening or when its dark,' said Karen.

'Why ever not?'

'I don't know, but I think it's a bit creepy.'

'Creepy? It's the safest place to be after your home,' said Alex. 'There are a lot more good souls than bad that have passed through its doors. I'll make a list of everything we need for this covert operation,' he added, smiling. 'We can't afford to be coming and going though, so we need everything to do the job with us on Friday night. It will be dark by 10 p.m., so let's make that our target time. What do you think?'

'Okay. It's a little later than I expected to be honest, but we need to see this through, or as the police say, "eliminate it from our enquiries", but most of all I want you to be right. But, if you don't mind me saying, you seem to have cracked this cipher very quickly. What makes you so sure that we're on the right track?'

'I don't think the cipher itself was meant to be difficult, but I think Charles Herle meant the finding of it to be difficult by disguising it within the letter with a different juice.'

'I do hope we're right,' said Karen.

'One of the advantages of keeping it low-key is that if we come up empty-handed, we only look silly in the eyes of a couple of people and not the whole community,' said Alex, and he then made his list and started the preparations for Friday night at the church.

Chapter 13

The Tunnel

THEY HAD both been looking forward to Friday night, but by the time Alex had said, 'Right, let's go', at 9.45 p.m., Karen was less enthusiastic and felt more like preparing for bed. Louise was staying at a girlfriend's house on a sleepover, so the opportunity for a quiet relaxing night was now. However, Karen hoped it would only take two hours tops to get this job done. After all, they were only lifting a broken paving slab to see what, if anything, lay beneath it. How difficult could that be?

Alex had already loaded up the SUV with an array of equipment, including spades, crowbars, trowels, some pieces of timber, a bag of sand, extension leads and lamps.

'Why do we need all this lighting?' Karen asked. 'Won't we be able to use the lights in the tower?'

'No, that's too risky,' replied Alex. 'I know the tower lights are quite dim, but if some of the locals see lights at night, when they shouldn't be on, they will be on to the police, and imagine how that would look in the local papers the next day: "Body snatchers found in Winwick church". He gave Karen a cheeky wink.

'Come on, let's get this done,' she replied.

They set off for the church in the SUV. When they reached Moorsdale Lane, adjacent to the church, they turned left into a small unmarked lane, then left again into Rectory Paddock. It was very secluded, surrounded by trees, but directly opposite the church tower door. The SUV was well hidden, which was the object of the exercise.

All the equipment needed fitted into the large toolbox. They each took hold of a handle of the toolbox and lifted it out of the rear of the SUV. Alex closed the hatch and locked the vehicle. They waited for a few cars to pass before they walked across the road and up the steps into the churchyard.

The imposing tower stood in front of them, leaving a dark shadow against the night sky. Normally, the exterior of the church would be illuminated at night, but a wiring failure had left the church in darkness for several months, which was in their favour tonight.

They moved along the front of the church and Karen jumped as a startled pigeon flew from an alcove in the north wall. As they approached the chancel door, Alex reached into his pocket for the church keys. As he did so, the security light above the door flooded the area.

'I forgot about the light. Let's just get in as quickly as possible and hope no one has seen us,' Alex said, as he unlocked both of the locks. They were inside within seconds and in total blackness, other than a shaft of light coming under the door from the security light outside. The light clicked off and suddenly they were in total darkness.

Alex opened the heavy inner door into the chancel and was hit by the familiar odour that all old churches emanate – a mixture of carpets, old stonework, flowers, furniture polish, and a musty hint.

'Put your flashlight on Karen, but use it to light the floor in front of you.'

'Okay,' she replied.

The temperature in the church was much cooler, so much so that they could see their breath, even in the dim light emanating from the downward-pointing flashlight beam, every exhalation seeming to create a plume of fog. They walked slowly on the heavy red carpet to the chancel screen, Alex dragging the toolbox on its wheels, then they stepped down into the new carpeted dais area. This was the area used for concerts, bands and choirs to perform on evenings of entertainment.

They were now in the nave of the church, and having passed down a couple more steps, were soon on the stone paved floor of the main aisle. At this point they lifted the toolbox and carried it to create as little noise as possible.

As they approached the tower, there was a rope strung across the screen entrance and a wooden sign tied to it saying, 'BELLS SET, PLEASE DO NOT TOUCH THE ROPES'. This sign at first glance seemed to be a permanent fixture, but it just unhooked from the other side of the screen and was then left to dangle on one side.

'Be careful on these steps,' warned Alex, as he led the way down and into the bell ringers' domain. Karen followed slowly, tightly holding on to the toolbox handle. The temperature seemed to be a couple of degrees lower in the tower, probably because there was no heating in there, unlike the main parts of the church.

They walked over to the north-west corner, where Alex highlighted the paving slab in question with his flashlight.

'It's just so inconspicuous,' said Karen.

'Yes, and that's how it's supposed to look when we've finished. In fact, if you don't mind taking a photograph, just in case we have any trouble putting the slab pieces together later.'

'Yes, okay. I'll turn the flash off and see if it works.'

'If you hang on a minute, I'll just rig my light up and you can take the photograph then.' Alex opened the toolbox and produced an extension lead, which he plugged into a socket by the tower screen. He then pulled out an LED spotlight on a small tripod, angled the head down, and turned it on. By angling the head down, it highlighted the area that they were interested in without illuminating the whole tower, which would show out in the nave and attract attention.

Karen took a string of photographs from different angles then viewed them on her mobile. She was quite happy with the results.

'You know, I reckon there used to be a small wooden cupboard or cloakroom here,' said Alex.

'Why do you think that?'

'Because if you look at the walls you can see a line of small holes going vertically on the north and west walls, with the remnants of wooden plugs. They were probably frame-fixing points for a very small timber structure. When you think about it, it makes sense; maybe the rectors of the day used it on a daily basis just to get to and from church when it was raining or snowing. A cupboard around the entrance would give a bit of privacy when climbing in and out, or for all intents and purposes it may have appeared as a locked cloakroom.'

'I see what you mean; but it would be pretty difficult lifting a heavy stone flag, particularly from the inside.'

'It would probably just have had a wooden hatch with a handle on the inside, and perhaps a pull ring on the outside,' Alex suggested. 'Who knows?'

'You've really got this worked out, haven't you?'

'I hope so. I really do.'

Alex then pulled out two crowbars and two good lengths of 75mm by 75mm timber battens. 'If we put these next to the slab, we can lift up the biggest pieces and place them on the timbers,' he suggested. 'It will be easier for us to move them afterwards. Okay?' Karen just gave a thumbs up as they both donned their fabric and leather-type industrial gloves.

If anyone saw us now, we definitely look like church thieves, Alex thought, as he took one of the crowbars and forced it into one of the cracks in the slab. He was very quickly able to lift a section of the slab, and immediately the air was filled with a very strong putrid smell of decay and dampness.

'Wow, that's really strong Alex.'

'Yes, that's the smell of history, of age and decomposition.'

'Yes, but decomposing what?'

'Don't worry,' Alex assured Karen, 'there have been no burials here for hundreds of years. Not that we know of anyway.'

'That's why I'm worried. It's the what we don't know bit.'

Alex managed to lever out the piece of slab, but not before Karen had used her crowbar to double the effort. Alex was now standing over the slab and had grabbed the piece with his gloved hands. He lifted it on to the waiting timbers just a few feet away.

'Oh my god, what's going on? What on earth is this?' exclaimed Karen.

Alex had placed the piece of slab down and they were now looking at the patch of earth that had been revealed. What they were looking at was a cross-piece of a substantial-sized flat-iron framework.

'Pass me your flashlight please Karen.' She handed it over and Alex pointed it through the gaps either side of the framework. 'I can't see the bottom, but it looks like some kind of tunnel. I think there are stone steps leading down.' *I knew it, I just knew it*, Alex thought, excitedly.

'It reminds me of an old castle dungeon cover that I've seen in Skipton Castle,' Karen said.

'I know what you mean, but churches tend not to have dungeons,' Alex said, smiling.

'I know that, but it looks like we could have found the infamous tunnel. According to folklore and legend there's a tunnel that runs for miles from here, or to here, supposedly used by Cromwell and the hierarchy in the English Civil War, and no doubt for a multitude of other reasons.'

'Well that's why we're here in this spot,' said Alex.

'I know, but to come straight to it like this it's just ...' Karen was lost for words.

'Hard work and research Karen. There's nothing lucky about this and, yes, I've heard those rumours too, but if this is a tunnel, I'd like to bet it goes to the location of the original rectory, which was over in what is now Rectory Paddock where we left the SUV.

'In the sixteenth century, when the country was going through the dissolution of the monasteries and persecution of Catholics, priests used to meet and hold mass in private at secret locations. All these locations had priest holes where they could hide when the authorities came searching. They also used tunnels to make good their escape, so they could have used the rectory or the church, and this could have been their escape route or hiding place, as well as a convenient mode of access.'

'It's fascinating,' said Karen. 'It really is.'

'Okay. Let's get the next piece up,' said Alex, gripping the second piece of slab and just managing to lift it across to its temporary home on the timbers.

'I can see why the slab may have broken in the middle,' said Karen. 'The metal framework beneath it has corroded in the middle and sagged. It's offered no support, and I guess over time with people walking on it, the slab has slowly cracked.'

'Shh,' said Alex, holding an upright forefinger across his mouth. In the distance, a police siren could be heard, which seemed to be getting louder and louder. He quickly unplugged the light, and they were sitting in total darkness. Alex pulled Karen closer and put his arm around her shoulder.

'We don't need to sit here in the dark Alex. We're not breaking the law.'

'All the same. Let's just give it a couple of minutes.'

The cars seemed to come to a halt just outside the church, on Moorsdale Lane. There were voices, and police radio messages could be heard loud on the still night air.

'What are we going to say?' asked Karen, but Alex gestured with his finger across his lips again.

'I don't think they're here for us. It sounds as if they've just stopped a car outside, but we should wait for a while before we turn the light back on.' Alex gave Karen a reassuring look, but doubted she could see him.

They sat there and waited in the dark, then suddenly there were slight scratching noises coming from the tunnel below, which gave both of them a start. Alex grabbed his flashlight, turned it on, and shone it through the metal grille down into the tunnel. He had a better view inside of the tunnel now that the tower was in darkness, as it accentuated the effectiveness of the flashlight.

'I can't see anything moving,' Alex whispered, 'but I'm sure there will be mice and all sorts down there. The stone steps seem to go down, then westwards towards Moorsdale Road. Looking at the bricks that the tunnel is made of, they look original Tudor. They're a smaller handmade brick; it's how they made them at the time. This was here before Charles Herle. Karen, I reckon we're in the right spot. Alex turned off the flashlight, leaving them in total darkness again.

There was still some activity in Moorsdale Lane, but car doors could be heard closing and at least two cars had driven off. Alex whispered, 'Let's wait a little longer before we put the light on just in case there's another car still there.'

He was correct; there was still one police car parked at the roadside and the officer was standing adjacent to his car, smoking a cigarette, no more than fifty metres away from the church tower.

Alex and Karen sat in silence. There was a pair of old wooden doors in the west side of the tower, and the only people with keys were the churchwarden and bell ringers. But it was the gap around the frame and any light seeping out that made Alex extra cautious.

They waited for what seemed an eternity until they heard someone close a car door, then speed off with sirens blazing. Happy that the coast should now be clear, they turned on their low-level light again. Although they had not yet removed half of the slab, they could already see the design of the metalwork below. The heavy metal grille sat in a frame, and the grille was hinged on the side that had been revealed.

They worked together to pull the other pieces of slab out and set them down in order with the others, like a heavy-duty completed jigsaw puzzle.

'The good news is that there doesn't seem to be any locking device, so we should be able to pull this open,' said Alex. They were both crouched over the grille at one end, with a grip on each side.

'Right, pull,' instructed Alex. They pulled with their combined force, and the grille lifted about two centimetres. In the process, the hinges made a very loud high-pitched metal on metal screech of the type that you hear in a mechanic's shop when they're tightening a wheel nut. It was very loud, then they were standing there for a moment in silence.

'Okay, let's hold it there,' said Alex, as he reached across to the toolbox and pulled out a couple of small blocks of wood about ten centimetres in length. He inserted one block across the corner of the frame below the grille, then did the same in the other corner.

'Okay, let it down slowly,' Alex said, and as they did, the grille briefly gave off another audible screech before it rested on the wooden blocks.

'Those hinges are well seized,' stated Karen. 'Have you got anything to free them off?'

'Not here, but Jill keeps a can of that spray lube in the vestry.'

'Spray lube? Really? It makes the vestry sound like a right den of iniquity,' said Karen, with a fake look of shock on her face. Alex couldn't help but snigger at Karen's comment.

'I'm coming with you,' said Karen. 'There's no way I'm staying here on my own.' They both made their way out of the tower through the nave and up into the chancel, using their flashlights to light the way. As they approached the inner door of the chancel, moving towards the vestry door in the entrance area to the right, the outside security light came on and flooded through the gap at the foot of the outer door.

'Stop. Shh,' whispered Alex. They could hear male voices outside; they were loud and slurred, perhaps people on their way back from the pub.

'It's okay,' said Alex. 'They've set the light off walking past. It's a bit of a cut through. Let's just wait for the light to go off.' The light was on for no more than a minute, then all was quiet again.

Alex used his latch key to open the vestry door, and walked through quickly, then opened the vanity unit door, which sat below the sink. Using his flashlight, he located the can of lube, closed the vanity unit door, and made his way out of the vestry.

'Did you get it?' asked Karen.

'Yes,' replied Alex. They closed the vestry door and made their way back through the church to the tower.

Crouching over the grille, Alex sprayed both hinges with plenty of lubrication. 'Let's just give it a minute,' he said. He looked at his watch; it was coming up to 11 p.m. 'I know it won't cover the noise that we're about to make, but it may help. When the clock starts to chime, we'll start working on this grille to see if we can get it lifted. Are you ready?'

'Yes, ready.'

'On the strike of every chime, we lift together,' Alex instructed. The clock chimed and they both lifted. The grille moved about another inch, but not with the same audible complaint. The lubricant seemed to be working, as they lifted on each chime. Then suddenly on the eighth chime the grille gave way and lifted all the way open, settling just past the vertical.

They could now see the full damage to the grille, as the corrosion to its centre had caused a belly in its shape, leading to a couple of fractures in the metal.

For the first time they could now see the size and layout of the start of the tunnel, which descended down a set of crude stone steps. It was perfectly circular, brick-lined and approximately one metre in diameter. It turned towards the west after approximately five metres, so their view was somewhat limited.

'Do you think it's safe to go down there?' Karen asked. 'What if the steps give way or something else happens?'

'I've not even said I'm going down there yet,' replied Alex.

'I'm not sure you should.'

Neither am I, but we've not done all this work to fall short now, thought Alex, before suggesting, 'I've got an idea. In the clock room there's a large length of rope. I'm going to go up there and bring it down, tie it on to one of the wall hooks that the bell ringers' ropes are fished through, then I'll tie the other end around my waist. You can release more rope as I descend.'

'Okay, it sounds like a plan, if you're happy to do it, but don't take any more risks than necessary. You're not doing this because you have to, you know that.'

'I know, but it's a need to know basis, and I need to know.'

Alex opened the door to the bell tower steps. He had originally planned to walk up the stone spiral staircase without any light at all, just by feeling with his feet and keeping a hand on the wall, but it was too difficult, so he used his flashlight. Each time he approached one of the small mesh-covered inset windows he turned the light off until he had passed by.

As he wound his way up the staircase there was a sudden scuffling noise just ahead of him. In his panic he nearly fell backwards, then as feathers fell across his face, he realised he had just disturbed one of the pigeons nesting on a window ledge. *Thank goodness for the mesh. Damn pigeons; I don't know which was more scared, me or the bird.*

Alex approached the clock room door, which was held secure by a simple metal hook and eye. As he lifted the hook the door swung open with a long, slow creaking noise. Scanning the floor with the flashlight, Alex spotted a large, dusty coiled-up rope, which by the looks of it probably hadn't been moved for several years. He picked up the rope, gave it a shake, then threw it over his shoulder, before going back through the door and making his way back down.

Karen was sitting by the tunnel entrance, wishing Alex would hurry up. She didn't feel comfortable; in fact, she was scared. She could still hear noises coming from inside the tunnel. *I guess it's rats or mice. I can't see much else living down there.*

She was relieved when Alex came through the tower door. 'Thank goodness. It's pretty creepy here on your own,' she said, as he came into the light. She could see the beads of sweat on his forehead. He looked tired and tense. 'Are you okay? she asked.

'I'm fine. I just want these documents, then I want to go home to bed, but I'll just take a minute to get my breath back.' He sat down beside Karen.

Karen looked at him. 'Why does this feel so wrong?' she asked.

Alex hesitated before answering. 'I don't know. We're on the brink of retrieving some historical documents, for which we have permission, but it still feels like we're carrying out some sort of desecration. I don't want to go down there Karen, but whether we find anything or not, we've seen it through, and we'll make it look like we've never been here.'

With that, Alex got to his feet, took one end of the rope and fished it through one of the metal wall loops. He took a piece of timber from the toolbox and placed it across the opening to the tunnel. He wrapped the other end of the rope around the timber, then around his waist and explained to Karen that for him to descend into the tunnel she had to feed the rope across the timber, but if he fell, his body weight should tighten the rope around the timber and stop his fall.

Karen gave him a kiss. 'Good luck. Don't come back empty-handed.'

Alex smiled. 'I'll try my best.'

'I know you will but please be safe. No risks.'

Alex descended into the tunnel with his flashlight on and with Karen feeding him the rope. At first it was easy, a little claustrophobic, but the steps were set evenly and seemed secure enough. He noticed that the further he went the tunnel went slightly wider. There were small alcoves in the walls every couple of metres, and Alex put his hand in one by mistake and could feel a waxy substance on the brick. As he looked closer, he could see what looked like candle wax, which had melted and run down the wall. There was even the remnant of a wick left in its centre. *Amazing. I wonder whether Charles Herle was the last person to light this candle.*

The tunnel now turned in a westerly direction and Alex could no longer see the light at the entrance, or Karen peering in. There was a further incline before the tunnel seemed to level out. He could now turn around and look in the direction of his travel. He shone the flashlight forwards as something scurried across his feet. *Probably a rat.* Then, to his disappointment, he noticed a pile – mainly bricks and some earth. The bricks from the wall and ceiling had caved in and the way through was blocked. Alex's heart sank. *After all this.*

He took his time assessing the damage and how safe he thought it was. There were protruding tree roots that were dripping ice-cold water but thankfully there were no signs or remnants of any interments.

The structure where he was standing and the tunnel that he had just passed down were in pretty good condition considering they had presumably been devoid of any maintenance work for hundreds of years. He noticed on the wall to his right that there was a small hook protruding from one of the seams in the brickwork. It looked possibly copper or brass, and it looked old. Alex scratched his head. *Could have been used to perhaps hold an oil lantern.* He inspected the brickwork above it and noticed a darkened area that showed up particularly on the mortar seams. *Could be soot deposits.*

Walking up to the blockage in the tunnel, he reached to the top and scraped away some soil, which only revealed fallen bricks. He pulled away a brick from the pile and immediately there was another brick, so he pulled away a few more. The bricks behind them seemed to be pretty solidly stuck at all sorts of peculiar angles; they wouldn't budge.

This blockage could go on for metres or further, but what if I'm just a few bricks away from seeing what's on the other side?

Alex stepped back from the blockage and turned around to make his way back up to Karen to tell her of his discovery. As he stepped forwards his foot was caught in a ring of the rope and he fell forwards on to it, grabbing it as he fell.

Karen, at the entrance, felt the rope tense and tighten around the timber. 'Alex! Alex! Are you all right?' She was shouting with deep concern in her voice, the acoustics in the tunnel producing a crystal-clear amplification of her voice.

Alex could hear the concern in Karen's voice. 'It's okay, I'm on my way up,' he shouted back.

At the tunnel entrance Karen was concerned not only for Alex but at the fact she had raised her voice and increased the possibility of being heard from outside. Meanwhile, Alex made his way up the stone steps and climbed out to where Karen was waiting.

'What happened?' she asked.

313

'I tripped over the rope, but it's okay, no harm done.'

'I take it the fact that you're empty-handed means you didn't find anything.'

'Correct. There's been a collapse at the point where the tunnel starts to level out. I removed a few bricks, but I need a hammer and a block of wood to see if I can burst through at the top.'

'Are you mad? This has gone too far and is far too dangerous as it is. We should call it quits now.' Karen was genuinely concerned.

Alex composed himself. 'I want to try to burst through the top of the blockage. I just need five minutes with my hammer and a block of wood. If I can't burst through, then we'll call it quits. We've come this far Karen, so it deserves one last chance.'

'It doesn't!' shouted Karen, and Alex hushed her immediately. 'It doesn't matter Alex,' Karen said in a quieter voice. 'I'm sure people would have heard me by now when I was shouting concern for my husband, thinking you had had an accident.' Karen was exasperated at Alex for not agreeing with her.

'I just need five more minutes, then we finish,' Alex said, taking hold of Karen's hands.

She thought about it, then replied, 'Okay then. But only if I come down with you.'

'No way.'

'Okay then,' Karen said, as she started to put some of the tools back in the toolbox.

'What are you doing?' Alex asked.

'I'm packing up,' came the nonchalant reply.

Alex grabbed Karen's arm. She looked down at his gloved hand around her wrist, then looked at him. 'Team Helsby is what we are, so we do this together or not at all.'

'I need you topside Karen in case something goes wrong. You can always go and get help. But if we're both down there and it goes wrong, we're finished; there's no one to help.'

'Well if it's that dangerous you shouldn't be going down there anyway, so as far as I'm concerned you can ...' Karen's next words were totally drowned out by the church bells chiming midnight.

When the bells had finished, Alex said, 'Were you going to swear then?'

'I did actually.'

Alex wrapped his arms around her. 'This is foolish but let's do this together.'

'Well, it's the only way it's going to get done.'

Team Helsby then gathered together what was needed and Alex descended into the tunnel first. He had thrown the rope into the tunnel with the other end still connected to the hook in the tower; it was a lifeline to the surface if they needed it.

'Just take it nice and easy,' Alex informed his wife. 'The steps are secure; they're just different sizes and shapes.'

'Okay.'

They were soon near the bottom of the tunnel entrance just as it turned west and started to level out. 'Right; on the next step you can turn around and look at me,' said Alex. Karen turned around and immediately over Alex's shoulder she could see the collapse in front of them, but before she had chance to speak, Alex pointed to the top of the mound.

'That's the area I'm going to have a go at,' he told her. 'Can you see the highest bricks right in the centre?' Karen nodded. 'Well I've already pulled quite a few bricks down from that area, but the ones that are left are pretty tight, so I was going to see if I could knock them through to the other side. They'll either go or the blockage is metres deep and they stay put.'

'That looks very dangerous,' warned Karen. 'They could be supporting whatever is above, so if you knock those bricks through you could cause a further collapse in the structure.'

'That's why I want you to step backwards on to the steps, so at least you'll have a chance to get away if it all goes wrong. You step back but keep your flashlight on the area so I can see which ones to hit.'

Karen had no time to argue, she just moved to the steps and was illuminating the brickwork as Alex had requested. He had a lump hammer in his right hand and in his left was holding a block of timber against one brick. He swung the hammer, and thought the brick moved slightly. He tried again, and it definitely moved this time. Now he resorted to lighter fast taps. The brick was moving, then all of a sudden it disappeared, and he could hear a thud as it hit something on the other side. The noise corresponded with a gust of foul-smelling air, which came rushing through the hole that Alex had just made, brick dust and dirt catching him clear in the face.

Alex turned away and stumbled towards Karen. 'Are you okay,' she asked, grabbing him by the shoulders.

'I just need a minute. A lot of dust was blown through.' Alex started rubbing his eyes.

'Wait,' Karen said. 'The dust will scratch your eyes, so don't rub them. Hold them open with your fingers to make them water.' Alex obeyed. 'Now close them.' As he did, tears ran down the sides of his face, and Karen then used the sleeve of her T-shirt to wipe the corners of his eyes. They repeated the process three more times before Alex felt that he was able to resume.

Back at the blockage Alex had further success at knocking bricks through to the other side. The hole was now much larger, so he grabbed the flashlight and shone it through the hole. The breeze through the hole was strong and foul-smelling.

Alex narrowed his eyes, and the first thing he saw was a narrow gangling tree root hanging down from the ceiling. Then, as he focused, he could see more and more of the tiny roots dangling, as they sought water that they couldn't find. Looking at the ceiling above he could see a large tree root running the arc of what used to be the tunnel brickwork, but had eventually given up due to the pressure from above and had grown around the tunnel from the other side, eventually bursting through. It was now sprouting a curtain of fine roots.

Then Alex thought he caught a glimpse of something on the floor at the side of the tunnel. It looked like an irregular-shaped mound of clothing that had been covered by centuries of dirt.

'What do you see Alex? You said you needed five minutes. We've passed that now.'

'The tunnel is clear on the other side. There are lots of tree roots hanging from the ceiling just above where the bricks have fallen in. About five metres in, on the floor, there's a mound of something, or maybe it's nothing. I can't see anything else in there. Come and see for yourself.'

Karen's curiosity got the better of her and she rushed over with her flashlight to look. She scanned the tunnel and could see what appeared as a mound of dirt-covered clothing, but her main concern was the tree root that was mimicking the shape of the tunnel roof just above her head and its curtain of cascading vein-like roots.

'That roof could come crashing down at any minute,' she said.

'Best I get in there quickly then and recover whatever is under that mound.'

'Are you seriously going to go in there?' Karen said with disdain in her tone.

'We can't leave that Karen. That could be our target.'

It took Alex no more than ten minutes to make a hole big enough for him to crawl through. Karen had tied the rope around his waist so they could always find each other in an emergency. He pushed his way over the mound of bricks and rubble, lost a bit of control and was unceremoniously dumped to ground on the other side, taking skin off his knuckles, knees and elbows, but worst of all taking the life out of his flashlight. *This is a nightmare. Come on … please work.*

Alex was banging the flashlight with his hand when suddenly it came back on. *The batteries must have been dislodged. Someone is looking after me today.* As he stood up, he felt the tree roots on the back of his hand and tickling the back of his neck, making him shiver, so he decided to crouch down and move towards the target and try to avoid any more contact with the creepy roots.

As he moved forward, he could see his breath intensified in the flashlight beam. *It seems much colder on this side of the blockage … and that smell …* All of a sudden, Alex was feeling light-headed. He was standing over his objective now, so he bent down and with both arms scooped it up. A powder puff of dust raised into the air, so as well as feeling light-headed, he had now inhaled the dust and had started to cough profusely.

He made his way back to the opening and shouted for Karen, who was right by the opening, so Alex passed the bundle through the wall to the other side, warning her of the dust. Suddenly he heard a strange high-pitched squeaking noise. He turned around. *Probably rats.* However, in the beam from the flashlight he could see that there were hundreds of bats flying towards him, then going away in a continuous loop. One bat made contact with his face and another hit the inside of his thigh. *This is a nightmare. I bet my coughing has set these bats off. That's it. I'm out of here.*

Alex started to crawl through the hole but in his panic the heels of his boots had kicked the tunnel roof on the other side of the blockage and a substantial amount of soil, stones and some bricks had landed on his backside and the back of his legs. There was a look of horror on his face. *I'm stuck and I can feel things crawling on my skin.* He was desperate, but trying not to panic, and he let go of his flashlight, which rolled down the heap of rubble and landed at Karen's feet.

She could see he was in trouble and had placed the bundle on one of the steps and approached him with urgency.

'There's a load of earth and rubbish just fallen on me and I'm stuck from the waist down,' Alex informed her.

'Give me your hands! Quick, give me your hands!' she screamed. They gripped each other's hands firmly and Karen pulled, but her hands slipped free as they were wet and very muddy. She tried again and the same thing happened.

'Grab the rope and I'll grab it too,' said Alex. 'There may be more purchase that way.'

They were both now holding the rope, Karen pulling with all her might, but she could feel the rope starting to slip. Tears ran down her face as the rope tore a layer of skin from the inside of her right palm. She could feel movement though, and with renewed energy she heaved with one final big effort. Alex came through the hole slowly and then was once again unceremoniously dumped headfirst down the bank of rubble to the tunnel floor, freshening up the new grazes on his body. But he didn't care. He stood up immediately and gave Karen a long kiss on the lips.

'Thank you,' he said. 'That was horrible being stuck like that. I'd never have got out of there without you.' Karen hugged him tightly without saying a word.

Then with a start Alex said, 'I must start filling that hole, so that the bats don't make their way through into the church.' He pulled anything off the pile in front of him just to fill the hole – bricks, stone, soil, even a bit of old tree root – then he packed as much muddy soil over his handywork as he could.

He was covered from head to toe in wet mud, and his denims were hanging off him at the waist due to their saturated state. He was a mess.

'Do you think we got what we came for?' Karen asked.

Alex looked at the sad-looking bundle on the step. 'I couldn't see anything else down there, and to be honest I don't ever want to come down here again. Let's get it to the surface then we'll find out.'

'Okay,' agreed Karen, and started to make her way up the steps.

She was very relieved when she stepped out of the tunnel and into the tower. She lay her precious cargo on the tower floor. Alex wasn't far behind and had somehow managed to carry the hammer, timber and flashlight.

As he climbed out of the tunnel, Karen looked at him and said, 'You should see your face. You look like a miner.'

He was standing there, shivering. 'I've got to take these wet trousers off. There are a pair of waterproof ones in the toolbox. Can you pass them over?' Karen looked in the toolbox and saw what looked like the item, rolled up with an elastic band around it. She removed the band and allowed the trousers to unroll. Even they were covered in dry mud from the last time they were worn. She looked at Alex, who had removed his boots and trousers, and was now standing there in his boxer shorts. He looked like he was brushing something off his legs.

'What is it? she asked.

'Woodlice. Lots of them.'

She pointed her flashlight at his legs. 'Oh god,' she said, 'they're on your fleece as well.'

Alex quickly removed his fleece, his shirt and his T-shirt, and was left standing in just his boxer shorts and socks, shaking. Once he had finished brushing himself down, Karen handed him the waterproof trousers and he pulled them on quickly. He puffed out his cheeks as the cold waterproof material touched his bare legs.

Karen had picked up his T-shirt and was turning it inside out and shaking it before giving it back to him. She did the same with the shirt and fleece. She could see he was beginning to warm up and the rigorous shaking had nearly stopped.

'Looking at your face now, if you were wearing a helmet with a lamp you would look like a coal miner,' she told him.

'Now that's a job I couldn't do. I have every respect for those guys,' Alex replied.

They decided that they were not going to investigate the bundle until they got home, and they just wanted to make sure the church tower showed no sign of their incursion. Alex had inserted a small piece of hardwood to sit in the belly of the grille and to offer support to its middle when the paving slab was refitted. It went back into position exactly as it came out, like an easy jigsaw puzzle, except now it was relatively level.

Any dust and debris lying around was brushed into the gaps in the cracks. The whole tower floor was brushed clean, which was no easy task, as there was a fair amount of mud, dust and woodlice, but when they had finished you would never have known that the slab had been lifted, never mind what lay beneath.

The rope was returned to the clock room and the lubrication spray put back in its place in the vestry. They quietly made their way to the church exit, carrying an addition to the toolbox, which could be something or nothing.

As they opened the door, they noticed the thick fog, and when they stepped outside the security light illuminated it, so it looked like very fine rain. Although it wasn't windy, the fog changed direction and seemed to swirl about around their faces and between their bodies as they made their way with difficulty down the path, through the churchyard towards Moorsdale Lane. The church bells chimed – it was 2 a.m.

There was no passing traffic, so they were able to cross the road easily and, more importantly, without being seen. They made their way to Rectory Paddock and the SUV, loaded up and drove home.

When they arrived, Alex reversed up the drive. Karen went into the house, turned the alarm off, then came back outside brandishing a clean pair of denims for Alex before helping to load the toolbox into the garage. Alex removed the waterproofs and was relieved to feel the dry denims against his skin, as the waterproofs had made him hot and sweaty.

They took the lid off the toolbox and the smell hit them straight away, making then both back up for a second. 'Guano,' said Alex.

'Bat droppings,' added Karen.

Alex lifted the bundle out of the toolbox on to the workbench. It was now under the lights and was just a mess of mainly heavy grey-coloured powdery-type substance. He used a small hand brush to brush the contents into a carrier bag that was attached to a nail on the end of the bench. As he cleaned it, he realised that it was a sort of thick canvas bag that appeared to be tied in a knot at the top. He carefully tried to undo the knot, but it just fell away in his hand and turned to dust.

'This is really strange,' he said. 'It looks like thick canvas, but it's just rotted to powder. The guano must have been keeping its shape, but at the same time just rotting it away.'

'Try using a paint brush,' Karen suggested.

'Yes, that's a good idea.' Alex then selected a clean one from a shelf above the bench. As he brushed away the remnants of the bag, there was no sign of any documents, just another kind of material.

'Touch this Karen. What does it feel like?'

Karen leaned over and touched the material with the end of her fingers. 'Do you remember the wax coats that were all the go a few years ago?' Alex nodded. 'Well that's what it feels like.'

'I must admit that's what it looks like,' agreed Alex. 'I'm just going to see if it will tear.' It wouldn't, so he used a small knife to insert a tiny slit, which he then made larger with his fingers. He was then able to tear the material. They were greeted by a sight they were hoping for – pages and pages of handwritten notes in a brown-coloured ink, probably written in feather quill.

Alex looked at Karen. 'We've hit the jackpot again,' he said, and they threw their arms around each other.

'I feel like crying,' said Karen.

'Well don't cry over these documents, you'll damage them.' Alex picked her up in his arms and spun her around.

They carefully tore away the rest of the material to reveal all the documents. They were different sizes, slightly different colours, some were frayed at the edges, some were even stained, but they all appeared readable, and considering the circumstances under which they had been kept were in remarkably good condition.

Alex picked the topmost document from the pile, then realised just how fragile it was, so he put it down on the workbench to read.

Lodge of Great Learning

The regular meeting of this lodge was held at Bewsey Hall in Warrington, Lancashire on 16th October 1646 at 4.30 p.m.

Brethren and visitors were recorded accordingly and signed as per the duty of their presence.

On approval of the records of the previous lodge meeting, Messrs Elias Ashmole and Henry Mainwaring were then regularly initiated into Freemasonry. The charges of which were delivered to both initiates who then took their places in the lodge as apprentices.

The laws and byelaws of the lodge set down by our founder Francis Bacon were explained to the apprentices.

Notices and news were read by Secretary James Collier.

A record of our appreciation has been accepted by the Ireland family for allowing us the use of this extravagant venue.

There were no apologies for absences.

Our apologies were given to the landlord of the Warrington Tavern for the change of venue for this meeting. This decision was made as a result of recurring outbreaks of the bubonic plague in the town.

The lodge meeting was closed with solemnities and all fellow brethren requested to dine forthwith.

James Collier, 16th October 1646, meeting closed 5.55 p.m.

The notes were recorded in a very fulsome fashion. At the start of every sentence, the first letter of each word commenced with a large swirling and overarching of the quill and, in some cases, too much ink had been applied, causing a blot on the paper. All the writing leaned to the right apart from the first letter of every line. A further document was attached with a list of signatories.

Richard Penketh, Warden
James Collier, Secretary
Richard Sankey
Henry Littler
John Ellam
Richard Ellam
Hugh Brewer
Elias Ashmole
Henry Mainwaring

Looking over Alex's shoulder, Karen said, 'Do you know much about freemasonry Alex?'

'Not a great deal. It's not really my thing, but from what I remember, Francis Bacon was a genius. He was a scientist and a philosopher, and at one point was Lord Chancellor. Elias Ashmole was a politician, an astrologer, an alchemist, and another brilliant brain. They were very important, influential people of their day.'

'In that case, the lodge was suitably named,' suggested Karen, before adding, 'Of course ... it's just dawned on me ... Elias Ashmole ... the Ashmolean Museum.'

'Correct; and a host of other things, such as being one of the Founding Fellows of the Royal Society.'

Karen grinned. 'I guess this is a valuable document then.'

'Historically priceless,' agreed Alex.

Karen looked at her watch; it was 2.55 a.m. 'Do you think we can leave the other documents until the morning? I'm absolutely bushed.'

'Same here. I think that's a good idea. Do you think we should leave the papers in here?'

'Yes. I wouldn't subject them to a warm house, not after they've been underground for over three hundred and fifty years. They need to be kept cool and dry, so if we can just wrap them in acid-proof paper and leave them on the bench here for now, then we can go through the rest in the morning.'

After taking care of the documents, the Helsbys went to bed, both very tired and in need of a lie-in the next day, so Karen set the alarm on her phone for   9.30   a.m.

Chapter 14

The Mysterious Documents

AWAKE AT 9.30 but still lying there at 10 a.m., Karen asked Alex, 'What was it like when you crawled through the hole in the tunnel?'

'It was horrible. It was cold, smelly and damp, but worst of all, I literally slid down the rubble on the other side, hit the floor quite hard and my flashlight went out.'

'Oh my god, I didn't know. You must have been terrified.'

'I was,' confirmed Alex, 'but when I looked up, I could see a small ray of light coming through from your side, so I felt a little better. Anyway, I banged the flashlight and it came back on.'

'Did you not see anything else down there?'

'Oh yes, those horrible roots dangling down from the roof of the tunnel where the main tree root had broken through. But to be honest I didn't really look, and when the bats turned up that was it for me … get the package and get out.'

Karen continued with the questions. 'Where do you think bats are getting in from then?'

'I don't know, and I don't want to find out.'

'I can't believe it. We went in there to look underneath a paving slab and found a medieval tunnel. You went metal detecting in a field and found an ancient safe full of treasure. The whole thing … it's so bizarre but so fantastic,' said Karen.

'I know. It's hard to comprehend, and I don't think it's finished yet. I mean, those freemasons meeting minutes, with names like Elias Ashmole and Francis Bacon as the founder … it's just pure history in its finest form. I really can't wait to look at the rest of those documents.'

'Same here,' agreed Karen, 'but showers first, then I'll make us some breakfast.'

'Thank you. And thank you for last night, or should I say this morning. I couldn't have done it without you,' Alex said, before kissing Karen on the forehead.

'I think I overcame a few phobias last night,' she said.

'Oh, which ones?'

'The being in church at night in the dark phobia, and the going down newly discovered tunnels that haven't been opened for hundreds of years that could possibly collapse at any moment phobia.'

'They're not phobias.'

'Not any more they're not,' said Karen with a snigger.

After showering and dressing, they sat at the dining table with tea, toast, and Alex's favourite lemon and lime marmalade. Karen looked at him and shook her head. 'You sure know how to show a girl a good time.'

'You loved it last night and you know it,' he replied.

'I'd rather be on a flight to Auckland to visit your sister for a few weeks.'

'Likewise, but while we're in the midst of all this ...'

'I know,' Karen said, 'but perhaps we could look at the idea again?'

Alex nodded his approval. 'Right, come on, let's get to it. I'm itching to look through these documents.'

In the garage, Karen very carefully removed the acid-free paper from the small sheaf of documents. Alex picked up the minutes from the freemasons meeting and placed them carefully to one side. The next piece of paper was like parchment and appeared to be blank. He held it up to the light and carefully studied it.

'I can't see anything on it, but we'll treat it as if there is something,' Alex said as he passed it to Karen, who placed it carefully on the workbench.

Alex looked at the next document. 'It looks as if we have a covering letter.' He picked the paper up, and again the lettering looked as if it had been written by quill using a similar light-brown-coloured ink, but the writing wasn't easy to read and looked as if it had been quickly written. He read it out loud:

'To my friend Edward Stanley I enclose a manuscript of my latest work and trust that the opportunity may arise for its production in the new world. Signed William Shakespeare November 15th, 1612.'

Alex exclaimed, 'I don't believe this. It's signed by William Shakespeare.' *Oh, my god. Is this for real? It's got to be authentic; it's got to be.* He passed the covering letter to Karen who was standing there open-mouthed. She turned the page over and showed him more writing in a different hand.

> *I Edward Stanley bequeath this play 'Cardenio' into the ownership of St Oswald's Church, Winwick via the trusted hands of the churchwardens.*
> *As of this day December 21st, 1612.*
>
> *Signed Edward Stanley*

Alex was stunned, in fact he was speechless; he couldn't even think. He had just seen reference to William Shakespeare and there was more to follow. He looked at the next page.

CARDENIO

Act One

Scene One

As they read on, there were then a series of people entering and leaving the scene. In fact, there were pages and pages of people doing the same. The play looked as if it had all been written at the same time. The writing seemed to roll over from one page to the next absolutely seamlessly and uninterrupted. Then, near the end, there appeared to be additions and alterations in the margin, all by the same hand. The pages were numbered by hand and each number was in a small circle. The last page was numbered 110 and headed 'Epilogue'.

There was more drama, about love and passion, hate and battles, loss then grief. At its conclusion, the document was signed: 'William Shakespeare, November 15th, 1612'.

Alex looked at Karen, who had been watching him, while reading the pages of the play. 'It must be a lost manuscript. I've never heard of *Cardenio*,' she said, smiling.

'If this is the real thing, and there's no reason to think it isn't, this is a priceless piece of classical historical literature, and we found it!' Alex shouted, and fist-pumped at the same time. The couple grabbed hold of each other and jumped up and down whilst rotating. They were overjoyed. They were ecstatic. *Life doesn't get any better than this*, thought Alex.

The garage door opened; it was Louise on her return from the sleepover the night before. 'I could hear you two from outside,' she said. 'What on earth's going on?'

'Oh, we came across a few old documents love,' said Karen. 'Come and have a look, and see what you think.'

The works of Shakespeare wasn't one of Louise's strong points but even she realised the significance of the play; however, the freemasons meeting minutes didn't even warrant a raised eyebrow.

Later that morning, Alex and Karen decided that the best thing to do was to photograph all the documents, download the photographs on to the laptop, then pack the documents safely away and leave them in the garage.

Before that, Alex called Reverend Jill, who, like Karen earlier, seemed to be somewhat lost for words, but managed to say that she would come round to see the documents at about 4 p.m. and hoped to pick Janice up on the way.

After downloading the photographs, Alex and Karen were in the study sifting through them, checking for clarity. 'I'm happy with these Karen. What do you think?' asked Alex.

'Yes, they're fine, and I think it's worth putting a copy of them on to a memory stick.'

'Yes, good thinking.' Alex took a memory stick out of one of the study drawers and plugged it into the laptop.

When it had finished, Karen unplugged it, and said, 'I'm going to pop this in the safe.'

'Okay, good idea,' agreed Alex.

Karen pulled open the door of a cupboard that contained several box files. She pushed a few of them to one side to make a clearing. The document safe was fitted in the wall, and it bleeped as she entered the four-digit code. The door swung open and the memory stick was safely deposited.

She turned to Alex. 'What are we going to do?'

'With regards to what exactly?'

'All of these amazing priceless documents that are in our garage.'

'At this point Karen, I'm not one hundred per cent sure. We may have to ask your colleague Angel to point us in the right direction, but not until we've spoken to Jill. I think they need to be passed over to the care of St Oswald's, but they will need to be authenticated first.'

Karen added, 'Then they will need to be stored correctly and securely under the right conditions: temperature, humidity and so on.'

Alex stood there thinking to himself. *There's an awful lot to do, but we have to wait and see what Jill and Janice want. The documents are feeling a bit like a hot potato at the moment.*

That afternoon Alex and Karen concentrated on carrying out some research on the internet. Alex had decided to look a little more into the freemasons minutes and Karen into the Shakespeare play and the Edward Stanley connection.

Louise went about her normal weekend tasks, such as tidying her room and loading the washing machine, this after being told in no uncertain terms that she must not tell anyone, even her best friend, about the documents or any of their recent finds.

Louise was her usual nonchalant self and had simply replied, 'Whatever.'

During his research session, Alex established that the Warrington Museum of Freemasonry had a framed facsimile of Elias Ashmole's diary entry from October 1646, the day that he was made a freemason in Warrington. The entry corroborated all the information provided in the minutes, but it was the minutes that provided those vital additional bits of evidence that had been missing, evidence that was needed to complete the picture. They gave the lodge name, the Lodge of Great Knowledge; the venue, Bewsey Hall; and the founder, Francis Bacon. This information had been a matter of conjecture and speculation for over three hundred and fifty years, but not for much longer. *But why did the minutes end up in our church safe*? Alex mused.

He decided to do some research into the list of attendees at the meeting. Fortunately, Jill had loaned him a copy of *The Register of Winwick Part 2, 1621–1660* many months ago. It was a spare copy, so she had said he could keep it as long as he liked. The register was a record of baptisms, marriages and burials in book form for the period.

To his astonishment, he established that a Richard Penketh was married at St Oswald's Church, Winwick on 20 September 1638. *Could this be Richard Penketh, the Warden?* He then found in the burials section that a James Collier was buried in St Oswald's churchyard on 16 August 1651, so this could be James Collier, the Secretary.

He then consulted a copy of *Winwick, Its History and Antiquities* by William Beamont, and found Richard Penketh and John Ellam amongst others who had signed a Protestation document in 1641 in the presence of Charles Herle. Such a document was a proclamation to God and the king to be a good Christian and subject. The names and the years were a good fit, so either of these gentlemen could have originally deposited the minutes in the church safe, probably because, in their opinion, it was safer there than in the home or office environment. However, the reason for the deposit, considering the condition of the church both before, during and after the Civil War, was difficult to understand.

Karen, meanwhile, had made inroads into the life of William Shakespeare. The suggestion that he had spent a lot of his early years in Lancashire and had an association with the Stanley family appeared to be valid and, in recognition of this, a multimillion-pound replica Shakespearean theatre had been earmarked for a site in Prescot, Merseyside, about twelve miles from Winwick. The discovery of the documents and the association between Shakespeare, the Stanleys and the region were the confirmation that people had been waiting for.

The Stanleys were a very strong aristocratic family with connections to the monarchy and the court as the Earls of Derby. The current and 19th Earl of Derby, Edward Stanley, coincidentally was living in Knowsley Hall at Prescot.

Taking a break from their research, Alex and Karen were in the lounge drinking tea. Alex said, 'So, it looks like we've proven by association that these documents appear genuine. They just need to be verified by an expert.'

After getting back to work, time passed quickly, and it was later than the Helsbys thought when the doorbell rang. Karen opened the door to find Jill and Janice on the doorstep.

'Oh, hi,' said Karen, sounding surprised. 'I had no idea it was that late. Please come in.'

'Thank you,' said Jill, and was followed in by Janice. Karen shouted for Alex to come downstairs from the study.

Jill and Janice were seated on the sofa when Alex walked into the lounge carrying his laptop. 'Good afternoon ladies,' he greeted them. 'Have we got some news for you.' He sat down next to Karen and they started from the beginning, relating all the events of the previous night's visit to the church, ending with the details of the documents.

Jill and Janice were dumbfounded. As if the tunnel under the church wasn't enough; to then find out the importance of the documents.

Alex said, 'I'll show you on the screen first, then you can come into the garage and look at the real thing.'

Jill and Janice both looked perplexed. 'Why are you keeping them in the garage?' asked Janice.

'Don't forget that these documents have been below ground for over three hundred and fifty years,' replied Alex. 'They will have become accustomed to that environment. Bringing them into a centrally heated house all of a sudden could potentially dry them out and turn them to dust. That's probably a bit of an exaggeration but it would do them no good whatsoever.'

Alex scrolled through the photographs. Jill was particularly interested. 'The Shakespeare documents are so valuable. You can tell it's his writing, and his plays always involve love, passion or death, with more than a hint of humour. The style reminds me of *As You Like It*. Everyone with the slightest interest in Shakespeare is going to want a copy of *Cardenio*.'

After Jill and Janice had looked through some but not all of the images, they wanted to see the originals. They were taken into the garage, where the documents remained in their pile on the workbench.

Alex warned them, 'I know that I've separated these pages in order to photograph them, but I recommend they're now handled with extreme care, as they're very fragile.'

Karen reiterated the concern. 'Yes, any unnecessary handling could cause considerable damage.'

'So, what's our next move?' asked Jill.

'We need to get them authenticated, and I guess also see whether we can get a valuation. I think they need to go to the Museum of Liverpool for that purpose,' suggested Alex.

'Have you heard anything from the museum about the Claybarn find?' said Jill.

'No, not yet,' replied Alex. 'They will take their time and do things thoroughly. I'll give them a call in the morning though, to see how things are progressing.'

'What are you going to do with all of the Claybarn finds and the documents from the church tunnel?' Jill asked.

'We could be talking about valuable items potentially worth millions of pounds here Jill,' said Alex, 'so we need to think about storage, insurance and any press releases. Which items, if any, are you going to sell to boost church funds?'

'It's a nice position to be in,' said Janice. 'We've struggled for all these years and now we have an abundance of riches.'

'I agree,' added Jill. 'Someone is looking after us, and you should be recompensed for all the work that you've done on our behalf.'

'Thank you, Jill, but believe me we don't want anything. That's not why we do it,' said Alex, as Karen took hold of his hand, indicating that she was in full agreement with him.

'Well I think you should get some recognition for what you've done,' said Jill.

'I don't think we want that either Jill,' interrupted Karen. 'We're very comfortable in what we have and what we do.'

'I understand,' said Jill, 'and I respect your wishes. We'll need to discuss the finds in an emergency church council meeting. The other members will need to know what's occurred. We have to be transparent.'

Well, if the police don't leak it to the press, all it takes is for one member of the church council to mention it to the wrong person and it will be front page news, Alex thought.

Jill continued, 'I think in that meeting I'll also have to recommend informing the diocese.'

Janice shifted uneasily, adding, 'There are some good people there that will advise us.'

'That's great,' said Alex. 'I was going to suggest that I hand everything over to you when all the finds are returned from the museum.'

'That's good of you Alex, and of course on behalf of the church I'll be delighted to accept. But if you don't mind helping me to secure some adequate safety deposit boxes,' Jill said.

'Not at all. In fact, I've carried out a few enquiries already and several of the national banks have safety deposit boxes in Manchester. We should be able to get the gold and silver items secured away pretty quickly but, like I said before, the documents, once verified, will need to go into a conserved environment, and I think that should be in the Museum of Liverpool.'

'Okay,' agreed Jill. 'Will you be able to take them on Monday?'

Alex nodded. 'Yes, I'd love to, apart from the fact that we're very anxious about having them in our home. The museum will give us the red-carpet treatment when they know what we're bringing in.'

'I can't believe this. Have we really got a missing Shakespeare play? The only one in the world?' asked an excited Jill.

'Yes, I think we have Jill, I really do,' replied an equally   excited   Alex.

Chapter 15

The Secret Revealed

ON MONDAY morning Alex, accompanied by Janice, took the valuable documents to the Museum of Liverpool. Alex had forewarned them of the visit, so he was provided with a parking place very near to the main entrance. The curator of the museum had made a room available specifically for their visit, complete with two members of staff to unpack and prepare the documents. She had also asked for permission to take a photographic copy of all the documents, so on Alex's suggestion, Janice had telephoned Jill to get this permission.

Other museum staff came into the room at various points for an historic viewing of documents that, as far as they were aware, no one had seen for at least three hundred and fifty years; documents so rare that they were being treated with absolute consideration with regards to safeguarding and conservation.

One member of staff was heard to say, 'Wait until Stratford and the other outfits hear what we have.' He was immediately ushered out of the room by an unhappy looking curator. He was of course referring to some of the major players in the William Shakespeare 'industry'.

One of the museum representatives had attempted to hand a receipt for the documents to Alex prior to their departure, but Alex insisted it be given to Janice as the representative of the church. He also asked for any future communications or correspondence with regards to the Claybarn find and the documents to be with Janice or Jill.

It was only on their way back home that Alex had started to feel the weight of responsibility being lifted from his shoulders – and it felt good.

The following morning, he called the museum to speak to Melissa Michaels for an update on the Claybarn finds. She explained that all the items would be listed on the national database that day, and suggested that he keep logging on throughout the day and eventually he would find the listing. During the conversation, she confirmed to Alex that all the items had been verified as authentic.

When Alex logged on to the database later that afternoon there were two or three colour photographs of each item, plus a description. All the items that were found in the safe were displayed, except the documents.

RECORD ID – LIV-18350A

OBJECT TYPE: CROSS

BROAD PERIOD: LATE MEDIEVAL

COUNTY: CHESHIRE

A 24-CARAT SOLID GOLD CHURCH CROSS ON A STAND WITH HALLMARK AND

ENGRAVED ON THE REAR: ST OSWALD. THIS IS AN OUTSTANDING EXAMPLE FROM A HIGH-QUALITY CRAFTSMAN JEWELLER. FURTHER ENGRAVED WITH A FINE FLORAL AND VINE DESIGN TO EACH ARM AND UPRIGHT TO THE FRONT.

HEIGHT 450MM

CREATED 20 MAY 2017

RECORD ID- LIV-18701B

OBJECT TYPE: FLAGON

BROAD PERIOD: LATE MEDIEVAL

COUNTY: CHESHIRE

A SOLID SILVER HALLMARKED FLAGON WITH A HOLLOW BASE, A STEPPED OUTER RIM, A LARGE GENTLY FLARING CUP AND AN OPEN-TOPPED SPOUT WITH HINGED LID AND CURVED HANDLE. THE EXTRAVAGANT FLEUR-DE-LYS AND LEAF DESIGN PASSES FROM ITS BASE TO ITS LID ALONG ITS HANDLE.

HEIGHT 300MM

CREATED 20 MAY 2017

RECORD ID-LIV-18772C

OBJECT TYPE: CIBORIA

BROAD PERIOD: LATE MEDIEVAL

COUNTY: CHESHIRE

TWO BAROQUE-STYLE SOLID SILVER HALLMARKED CIBORIA CUPS WITH COVERS. THE LID IN EACH CASE SURMOUNTED BY A SOLID SILVER CROSS. IN THE BASE AT THE FRONT IS A RUBY GEMSTONE WITH A HEIGHT OF 15MM AND A WIDTH OF 10MM. ST OSWALD ENGRAVED ON THE REAR OF EACH BASE. TWO FINE EXAMPLES OF THE PERIOD.

HEIGHT FROM BASE TO TIP OF CROSS 175MM

CREATED 20 MAY 2017

RECORD ID-LIV-18779D

OBJECT TYPE: CHALICE

BROAD PERIOD: LATE MEDIEVAL

COUNTY: CHESHIRE

FOUR BAROQUE-STYLE HALLMARKED SOLID SILVER CHALICES. IN THE BASE AT THE FRONT IN EACH CASE IS A RUBY GEMSTONE WITH A HEIGHT OF 15MM AND A WIDTH OF 10MM. ST OSWALD ENGRAVED ON THE REAR OF EACH BASE. FOUR FINE EXAMPLES OF THE PERIOD.

HEIGHT 200MM

CREATED 20 MAY 2017

RECORD ID-LIV-18805E

OBJECT TYPE: WAFER BOX

BROAD PERIOD: LATE MEDIEVAL

COUNTY: CHESHIRE

A HALLMARKED CIRCULAR SOLID SILVER WAFER BOX WITH HINGED LID. ST OSWALD ENGRAVED ON THE REAR OF ITS BASE. A FINE EXAMPLE OF THE PERIOD.

HEIGHT 75MM

CREATED 20 MAY 2017

_____

This was fantastic news for Alex. *This is what I've been waiting for. They're all authentic and super-valuable and I reckon the documents are worth just as much, if not more.*

That night, the church held an emergency council meeting in the church hall. Reverend Jill had asked for full transparency on the circumstances surrounding the finds, so Alex told it exactly how it was, even down to cooking a piece of paper in the oven to reveal a letter and the sanctuary cipher. All the church council members were amazed at the depth and value of the finds, which resulted in a congratulatory and cheerful mood.

When it came to the subject of informing the diocese and the press, the mood changed. Janice was still concerned about the lifting of the stone slab to reveal the tunnel, which technically should only have been carried out with a faculty from the diocese. Jill again had to assure her that it was carried out in an emergency due to the damage to the slab and the fear of a health and safety incident, which wasn't untrue, and the finding of the tunnel was a mere consequence. She went on to ask Janice to retrospectively apply for a faculty for the work due to a health and safety risk, and Janice seemed much more at ease once this was suggested.

Alex got the meeting back on track when he produced photographs on his laptop of the Claybarn and church finds. He was asked numerous times about the finds and then about the tunnel that he had found beneath the church. The council members were totally taken aback.

He then showed the video footage that Thomas had taken of the opening of the safe and, as each item was revealed, the council members were transfixed, as they huddled around the laptop. There were quite a few 'oohs' and 'aahs' to be heard. Several had tears in their eyes as it slowly dawned on them that their beloved church had probably been saved as a result of the finds.

As composure returned to the group, they went on to agree that unless otherwise advised by the diocese, they would release a press statement indicating what had been found, but not being specific as to where it was found. This meant not giving away the location of the Claybarn find or the church's secret tunnel.

The members went on to agree that having a safety deposit box at a bank to hold the silver and gold items was a good idea. There was initially some displeasure at the suggestion of keeping the documents at the museum, and some of the members thought that it would be a good idea if all the finds were retained together in the same place, so that they were fully under church control. However, when Alex explained the requirements under duty of care to ensure that provision was made to aid conservation of the documents, and such factors as humidity, temperature and light etc., that were a crucial part of the conservation process, they finally agreed with him. One of the members, an ex-solicitor, said he would look into the legal aspect of holding such valuables, and the associated insurance requirements and costs.

It took a few weeks to hear back from the museum, where the tunnel documents had been looked at by experts within the Shakespeare and freemasonry fraternities. When they had finished their investigation, they stated that, as far as they were concerned, the documents were authentic. It was mind-blowing news that caused a considerable stir. Over the coming weeks, word spread through the community about the amazing finds connected to St Oswald's Church, then it soon became national and even international news.

The press was persistent, showing up whenever the church was open, and even attending services on a Sunday morning and a Tuesday evening. They all wanted to know who had found 'St Oswald's treasure' as they called it. They all knew what had been found – it was all listed in the press release – but the burning issue now was who had found the treasure and what was their story? The press had been camped outside the rectory for several days, and Jill was finding it impossible to go about her business, the strain beginning to tell.

Alex had just come off the telephone to Jill and was sitting in the kitchen with Karen. 'This isn't right Karen. Jill is being hounded by the press, wanting to know who found the St Oswald's treasure,' he said with a sarcastic grimace. 'They're camping outside the rectory, just waiting for a story.'

'Well, give them their story. They're not going to go away until they've found out who discovered it and where.'

'But they've already had a press release. That should be enough for them.'

'Well it obviously isn't. They need a face to the story. They obviously know it wasn't Jill who found the items, so they want to speak to who did.'

Alex thought about this. 'The last thing I want is the press hanging around our house, peeping in at us with their long-lens cameras.'

'Then you do your talk to the press at the rectory or the church. They don't need to know where we live.'

'It's easy for them to find out where we live. They're journalists, it's what they do.'

'All the same. I think you should give Jill a call and speak to her about it,' suggested Karen.

Alex called Jill and, as a result of the conversation, they agreed that a press conference should be carried out in the church hall, along with a representative of the diocese's legal department to deal with any difficult questions.

The following day at 2 p.m. the masses from the local and national press and news agencies gathered in the church hall. Outside there were TV crews with large satellite dishes fixed to the top of their mobile news vehicles. It was chaotic, but fortunately the local police had been pre-warned about the event, so they were on hand to keep local traffic moving and ensure order was maintained.

During the pre-press conference meeting the church team had agreed not to tell lies exactly, but to be economical with the truth. They wanted to keep the location of the Claybarn find and the church tunnel confidential, thereby giving the appearance that all the items were found together in a local field. The church council and the rector were not happy about disclosing a tunnel beneath the church at this point, for fear of enthusing treasure hunters, adventurists or people who may just force entry to search for themselves.

The press conference started promptly, with Jill introducing Tom Steele representing the diocese, Janice Wainwright the churchwarden, Alex Helsby from the church council and finder of the so-called St Oswald treasure, and a surprise late addition, Melissa Michaels from the Museum of Liverpool.

Jill commenced with a synopsis of events surrounding the finds and their current status with regards to authenticity. Melissa Michaels gave an update confirming the authenticity of the documents and the church relics. She was pushed for a valuation, even though she wasn't an expert, and eventually stated, 'It's impossible to put a price-tag on something so valuable, in particular the Shakespeare play.'

'Give us something please Melissa,' shouted an angry reporter from the rear of the room. 'Are we talking about millions or what?'

'Yes,' replied Melissa.

Hearing someone say that in an official capacity for the first time was a shock to Alex and Jill, who turned to look at him. Alex looked as shocked as she felt.

'Where is the treasure now? Can we see it?' the same reporter persisted.

'No, I'm afraid not,' said Jill. 'All the items are in a safe and secure place awaiting valuation, but there are plenty of photographs available, so please help yourself.'

It was at this point that a few of the reporters started to ask about the circumstances of the find, so Alex referred them to the press release, but they wanted more. They wanted to know about the safe, and where it was now. Where was it found? How was it opened? Alex didn't give away the location of the find, and they assumed that all the finds had come from the safe. Jill confirmed that when she first saw the safe, she recognised the St Oswald King of Northumbria symbol on its door.

They also wanted to know what the connection was between St Oswald's Church and William Shakespeare. Jill went on to mention that Shakespeare was supposedly a friend of William Stanley, and that the Stanley's (Earls of Derby) were benefactors to the church in the late medieval period, and indeed had provided eight former rectors of St Oswald's Church, and that the letter now proved this relationship.

With regard to the masonic minutes and Elias Ashmole, Jill confirmed that subsequent enquiries had revealed that there were two people at the time who were members of the church and had the same names as the Warden, Richard Penketh, and the Secretary, James Collier. She went on to point out that it was a good place to keep documents for a very secretive organisation, and she raised the question as to whether the rector at the time, Charles Herle, would have been aware.

The reporters simultaneously commented that they had not seen the letter she had previously mentioned and one of them asked whether this letter had been found in the safe. Jill stalled at this point, realising that she had inadvertently let the cat out of the bag, and she couldn't and wouldn't lie now.

At this point, Tom Steele from the diocese interrupted and asked for any other questions, but the reporters were not going to let this go, and fired the question again at Jill: 'Was the letter found in the safe?'

Alex wrote on the notepad in front of Jill: 'Shall I tell them?'

Jill nodded, and reluctantly and said, 'Yes.'

So, Alex went through the whole story uninterrupted, then suffered a barrage of questions at the end. The reporters made Alex look like a gambler; he had gambled with the letter by putting it in the oven to reveal the words, and he had gambled by digging up a stone slab in the church. Alex pointed out that they were educated gambles based upon research and historical knowledge, and that they had been correct.

As the meeting started to become a little heated, Jill brought it to a rapid close by informing the press that any further developments would be forwarded by email if all attendees could leave contact details. Some of the reporters were not happy, but that was all they were going to get.

Before he left, Tom Steele took Janice to one side to question her about the lifting of the stone slab without a faculty. Jill overheard the conversation and stepped in to inform him that, yes, it was the point in the church that Alex had identified as the location he believed the documents to be hidden, but it was a health and safety trip hazard, so she had asked him to try to fix it before there was an accident. Tom Steele looked sternly at both women for a second, then he broke into a smile. 'Good for you. Good for you. But don't forget the retrospective faculty application.'

Over the next couple of weeks, all the other items found, such as the coins, musket balls, stirrup and musket support iron, were identified, listed on the museum database, then collected by Alex. He had plans to have them all displayed in the church.

Jill and a member of the diocese had attended the Museum of Liverpool to collect the valuable items and take them to secure storage. They had been valued at £1.25 million. The masonic and Shakespeare documents were impossible to accurately value, but one expert on Shakespeare said that if the *Cardenio* manuscript came up for auction it would sell for millions.

It was front page news, and everyone connected with journalism seemed to want an interview, either with Jill to find out what the church was planning to do with its new-found wealth, or with Alex to get the unabridged story of how it all came to be – and that included him, Karen, and how they came to be. No stone was left unturned, but the Helsbys had no skeletons in the closet, so they just sat tight and hoped that eventually the furore would die down.

Alex and Karen Helsby were now the new wonder couple of the time – Mr and Mrs Indiana Helsby – named after the fictitious adventurer. Understandably, this started to become very embarrassing for the normally quiet and understated couple, and once all their interviews and meetings were completed, they were planning an escape to New Zealand for a month to visit Alex's sister.

The Shakespeare and masonic documents had been retained by the Museum of Liverpool in secure storage, on the understanding that they could have exclusive display rights, pending agreement with the church.

Meanwhile, Jill and the church council were presiding over which item or items of silver to put up for sale to clear the long-outstanding church debt, and they were consulting with a local auctioneer.

The exact location of the secret tunnel beneath the church had not been revealed, although it didn't take long for it to become common knowledge. This led to a dramatic increase in the number of visitors to the church, to the point where additional volunteers were being sought to deal with the crowds.

In some quarters, Alex was vilified in the press for the way in which he had supposedly ridden roughshod over archaeological items, such as the baking of the old document that had been written in orange juice ink and the cutting open of the safe. This attack was very upsetting for him, Karen and the family at the time, and all he could do was defend himself in the only way he knew, by pointing out that he had got the required results. The positive opinions started to gradually outweigh the negatives, and Alex and Karen once again became considered as Mr and Mrs Indiana Helsby.

The old safe had remained in the Helsby's garage, and there didn't seem to be any prospect of it going anywhere else. Also, the piece of blank paper that had been found in the church amongst the other documents was in fact blank, but this time Alex had not baked it in the oven to find out, he simply asked Angel to look at it instead.

Alex had spoken to Les Pritchard and his wife, thanking them immensely for giving him access to their land and helping as much as they did. They reiterated that they did not want any mention of their name or the name of the field where the finds had been made to come out. Alex had to point out that this information was also in the hands of the local police and the Museum of Liverpool from when he reported the finds. Les accepted this, but would be going ahead with security improvements to the fence line around a lot of his land anyway. Les also mentioned that he had heard nothing further from the ex-employee that he had let go after he was found to be nighthawking at Claybarn Field.

Ian Wright, the nighthawk from Moors Field, whose pregnant wife had died in a car accident, was now off crutches and had some part-time work. Jill had bumped into him at the local shop on more than one occasion and, as a result, had started to visit him at his home. He subsequently became the latest addition to St Oswald's congregation and was slowly beginning to take a more active part in the church, and was enjoying helping Janice as a churchwarden's assistant.

Angel had also asked to be kept out of the picture for fear of reprisals from her employer. It was therefore presumed by the press that Karen, being an employee of the museum in Warrington, had herself carried out the investigation into the invisible ink letter. This was an allegation that she did not deny, for Angel's sake. In order to keep her own job at the museum, Karen stated that she had carried out the works in her own time after completion of her normal shift.

Alex's brothers and son were also happy to be kept out of the limelight. Louise, after initially being quizzed by her school mates, was slowly becoming accustomed to seeing her parents' names in the newspapers, and on occasion seeing her father on the television. But Louise being Louise, she took it all in her stride and just carried on. However, she did cringe when she first saw mention of her parents with the tagline: 'Mr and Mrs Indiana Helsby'.

Alex and Karen had started to receive email and traditional mail via the church and the rectory. People wanted help finding long lost treasures that were missing from their church, or wanted them to investigate local folklore myths or even rumours about buried treasure. A couple from the US, and a church in Australia had even gone as far as offering to pay for flights and accommodation, just to get Alex and Karen to work with them.

By October, after a lot had happened to the Helsbys over the previous six months, they had received significant appearance payments and were still in demand for interviews from TV, radio and the press. It was as if their lives had been put on hold for months whilst they dealt with the fallout, and there didn't seem to be an end in sight.

Karen put her foot down and decided it was time to book their flights to New Zealand. Everything else could wait until they got back. She had plenty of time off due to her, which had been enhanced by time rolled over from the previous year. And, of course, Alex had plenty of time on his hands – he was, after all,   retired.

Acknowledgements

I would like to express my most sincere thanks to the following who have assisted me, knowingly or otherwise, with the writing of this book:

Rev. Canon June Steventon (St Oswald's Church, Winwick)

Christine Melia

Edward and Sue Fairclough

Warrington Museum of Freemasonry

Warrington Museum and Art Gallery

Museum of Liverpool

My son Chris and daughter Emma

My brothers John and David

Editor Ivan Butler

And finally, my wife Janet for her friendship, love and support

Printed in Great Britain
by Amazon

22958646R00215